EIGHT O'CLOCK TALES

Enid Blyton

EGMONT

EGMONT

We bring stories to life

First published in Great Britain 1944 by Methuen & Co Ltd
This edition published 2008
by Egmont UK Limited
The Yellow Building, 1 Nicholas Road
London, W11 4AN

Enid Blyton ® Copyright © 2008 Hodder & Stoughton Ltd

ISBN 978 1 4052 3975 2

www.egmont.co.uk

A CIP catalogue record for this title is available from the British Library

Typeset by Avon DataSet Ltd, Bidford on Avon, Warwickshire
Printed and bound in Great Britain by the CPI Group

5746/18

MIX
Paper
FSC FSC® C018306

CONTENTS

The Good Turn

Old Mr Turnabout was always doing good turns to people. He was a nice old fellow, very poor, but always willing to help anyone. You would be surprised at the number of good turns he did in a day.

He would help a child across the busy road. He would take a bundle from a tired washerwoman, and carry it for her. He would take anybody's dog for a walk. Really, he seemed to spend his time doing things for other people.

He was a very happy man, for he had dozens of friends. One of his friends was little Billy Smith, the small boy next door. Billy often used to see Mr Turnabout doing his good turns, and he always knew what the old man was going to say when people thanked him for his help. He always said the same thing: 'Don't thank me for the good turn I've done you! Just pass it on!'

That was a strange thing to say, wasn't it? 'Pass it on!' Billy asked him about it one day.

'Why do you ask people to pass your good turns on?' he asked.

'Because the world would soon be full of good turns if we all passed them on!' said old Mr Turnabout. 'Then we should all be happy and friendly, shouldn't we? And that would be very nice.'

'Well, when *I* do a good turn to anyone I shall say the same as you do,' said Billy. 'I shall tell them to pass it on!'

'Yes, do!' said Mr Turnabout. 'And you'll notice a very strange thing, Billy. Sooner or later your good turn will come back to you! Yes, it will! It will be a different good turn, but it will be the one that you began!'

Billy thought that was very odd – but old Mr Turnabout knew what he was saying. And this is the tale of Billy's good turn and how it came back to him. Just listen!

The very next day Billy went to play with Wilfred, a great friend of his. They played marbles, and had a grand time. Then they thought they would go and call on Timothy, who lived in the next street, and show him their marbles. So off they went – but dear me, on the way there Wilfred's very best marble, a great big one of blue glass with pink stripes inside it, rolled down a grating into the cellar of a shop.

Wilfred stopped at once and looked through the grating in dismay. Now what was he to do? The shop was empty and locked up, for nobody lived there.

'That marble has gone for ever!' said poor Wilfred, almost ready to cry, because it really was a splendid marble. 'The shop is locked up and empty, and there is no way of getting the marble.'

But Billy had an idea.

'My daddy knows the man who has the keys to the shop,' he said. 'If I ask him perhaps he'll ask for the keys so that I can get your marble for you. I could unlock the shop, go down to the cellar and find it.'

'Oh, Billy, but it would be dark down there and lonely,' said Wilfred, looking at his friend. 'Wouldn't you be frightened?'

'Only a bit,' said Billy. 'Anyway, I'll try, Wilfred. As soon as my daddy comes home tonight I'll ask him.'

Billy kept his word. He told his father about Wilfred's beautiful marble and how it had dropped down the grating, and he asked him if he might go and get the keys from Mr White, the caretaker down the road, and find the marble for Wilfred.

'If you like,' said his father. He wrote a note to Mr White and gave it to Billy. The little boy ran off to Mr White's house, and in a minute or two he had the key of the shop in his hand. Good! Now he could go and hunt for Wilfred's marble!

It was getting dark so he took his torch with him. He unlocked the door of the empty shop and went inside. It was dusty and smelt stale and nasty. Billy found the steps that led down to the cellar and climbed down them. The cellar was full of spiders' webs and he didn't like it at all. But he really must find Wilfred's marble. He flashed his torch here and there, and at last found the blue marble in a corner. He picked it up, put it into his pocket and went up the steps again. In a minute or two he was out of the shop and was giving back the key to Mr White. Then he ran to Wilfred's house with the marble.

'You *are* a brick!' said Wilfred, delighted. 'See, Billy, do take one of my little green marbles for getting back my big blue one. You *did* do me a good turn!'

'No, thank you,' said Billy. 'I don't want a reward for doing a little thing like that, Wilfred. But you might pass on my good turn to somebody else. See? Just give somebody a helping hand when you can. It's a nice feeling – and tell them to pass on the good turn, too, won't you?'

'Yes, I will,' said Wilfred. 'It's a good idea.'

The next day Wilfred was running to buy some sweets from the sweet-shop when a lady in front of him slipped and fell. The bag she was carrying burst open and everything fell out. Papers went flying in the wind, books tumbled out, pencils and pens clattered on to the pavement.

'Oh, dear!' said the lady, and tried to clutch at her papers.

'I'll help you,' said Wilfred, remembering that he had a good turn to pass on. So he rushed after the flying papers, picked up all the other things, put them into the bag and handed it to the grateful lady.

She opened her purse to give him a coin, but Wilfred wouldn't take it.

'No, don't give me anything, please,' he said. 'I'm only passing on a good turn. Will you pass it on to somebody else?'

'What a splendid idea!' said the lady, very pleased. 'Yes, I'll certainly pass it on!'

It wasn't long before she was able to keep her word. As she hurried home that evening she saw an old woman standing at the edge of the pavement waiting to cross the road. There was a great deal of traffic rushing up and down the street and the old lady didn't quite like to cross, even when there was a clear space.

The young lady went up to her and took her by the elbow.

'Let me help you over,' she said. 'You'll be quite safe with me!'

She took the old woman safely across, and smiled at her kindly.

'That was a good turn you did to me, my dear,' said the old woman gratefully. 'Thank you.'

'Then pass it on to somebody else!' said the young lady. 'Don't forget! Pass it on!'

The old woman didn't forget. She kept wondering and wondering how she could do a good turn to someone, and at last her chance came.

Mrs Jones, her next-door neighbour, hung out her washing on the line, and then went off to do her shopping. The old woman happened to look out of her window and was just in time to see the washing-line snap in two! Down went all the clothes in a heap!

'Oh my! Oh my!' said the old woman in

dismay. 'Look at Mrs Jones's fine washing! It will all get dirty if something isn't done at once. I'll hurry round and pick it all up myself. I've got a good turn to pass on, and that shall be it!'

She went round to the next-door garden and unpegged all the clothes from the broken line. She was just gathering them all up when Mrs Jones came back from her shopping and saw what she had done.

'Oh, you kind soul!' she said. 'Thank you very much indeed. That's a great help to me. You *have* done me a good turn today! I should have been miserable if I'd come back and found I had all my washing to do again. Thank you for your very good turn!'

'That's quite all right,' said the old woman, pleased. 'Just pass on the good turn, will you?'

'I certainly will!' said Mrs Jones.

She didn't forget. She looked out for a chance to do a good turn and it soon came. Old Mr Lacy across the road was in bed with a bad cold, and Mrs Jones thought she would make him some good hot soup and take it to him last thing at night, so that he could have it before he went to sleep. So she carried him a basinful that night and he was delighted!

'This is really very kind of you,' said Mr

Lacy, gratefully. 'I shall enjoy the soup so much, and I am sure I shall have a good night after it. Many, many thanks, Mrs Jones. I hope I shall be able to return your kindness some day, for this is a real good turn you have done me.'

'Well, pass it on!' said Mrs Jones, laughing. 'It's a good idea to pass kind turns on, isn't it, Mr Lacy!'

Now Mr Lacy lay in bed and thought about what Mrs Jones had said. He wasn't usually a very kind man. He was really rather mean. But now that he had plenty of time to think about things, he wished he had done more good turns in his life.

'Well, it's not too late to begin,' he said to himself. 'There's heaps of time to do plenty of good turns even though I am an old man. Now what shall I do? Who is there that I can do a good turn to?'

Mr Lacy had a toyshop: two people worked for him, a girl in the shop and a man who did odd jobs, delivered parcels, mended broken toys, cleaned the window, did the books, and many other things. Mr Lacy thought about him.

'Smith will have had twice as much work to do since I've been away with this cold,' he thought. 'He is a good workman. I think I will do him a good turn. I will ask him if he has any children and I will send a nice toy to each of them. That's how I shall pass on the good turn that Mrs Jones did me.'

He felt quite excited about it. He stayed in bed three days more and then went back to his shop. The man, Smith, had helped the young girl in the shop, and had done all his own work and Mr Lacy's work too. Mr Lacy was pleased.

'Have you any children?' he asked Smith.

'Yes, one boy,' said Smith, surprised. 'He is eight years old and his name is Billy.'

'Oh, I was hoping you had three or four children,' said Mr Lacy, quite disappointed. 'I wanted to send them each a toy. Well, as you've only one child, Smith, you must choose him a very, very nice toy. What do you think he would like?'

'Oh, Mr Lacy, how kind of you!' said Smith, surprised and pleased. 'Well, there's one thing my boy would be so pleased to have, and that's a good clockwork engine. He's just broken his, and he's so miserable about it. It would be a real good turn to him if you'd let him have another engine.'

'I want to do a good turn,' said Mr Lacy, delighted. 'See, here is the best clockwork engine in the shop, Smith, and take two carriages and a signal with it. Tell your boy I'm pleased to do him a good turn, and say to him: "Pass it on!"'

Smith was very anxious to get home that night. Whatever would Billy say when he saw what he had brought him! The little boy had been very sad over his broken engine, but now he would be happy. Smith did up the engine, the two carriages and the signal in a big parcel and ran home all the way that night!

'You're all hot and out of breath, Daddy!' said Billy in surprise. 'Why did you run?'

'Because I have a lovely surprise for you!' said his father, smiling. 'Undo the parcel and look inside.'

When Billy saw the new train and fine signal he was overjoyed. 'But did you *buy* it for me, Daddy?' he asked.

'No,' said his father. 'Mr Lacy said he wanted to do somebody a good turn, so he asked me to take this home for you. But he said I was to say to you: "Pass on the good turn!"'

Billy looked at his father in surprise and said: 'Oh, how funny! That's what I said to Wilfred the other day when I got his marble for him out of the cellar of that empty shop. Do you suppose it's my good turn come back to me, Daddy?'

'Well, that's a funny thing!' said his father. 'I wonder if your good turn *has* been passed on from one to another and has come round to you again. We'll find out! First of all you must ask Wilfred who it was that he did *his* good turn to.'

So the next day Billy asked Wilfred.

'Oh, I picked up all the things that fell out when a lady's bag fell open,' said Wilfred. 'I don't know who she is, but I see her every day. We could ask her if she passed on my good turn, if you like.'

So they waited for her that day, and when she came down the road as usual, Wilfred stepped up to her and asked her very politely.

'Oh, I remember!' she said, smiling. 'Yes, I did pass on the good turn! I helped an old woman across the busy road just there. It was just about this time of day, so maybe she is doing her shopping again. Look! I do believe that is the old lady over there! Yes, it is! We'll go and ask her if she passed on the good turn.'

When they asked the old woman, she nodded her head and smiled. 'Oh, yes,' she said, 'I did pass it on! Of course I did! I picked up all the washing when my next-door neighbour's line broke.'

'We'll go and ask her if *she* passed on the good turn!' said Billy, feeling very much excited. How wonderful that his good turn should have started so many others!

So they went with the old lady to Mrs Jones and asked her the great question – had she passed on the good turn?

'Of course!' she said. 'I took some hot soup to the old man across the road. If you want to ask *him* about it, you will have to go to the toyshop in the next street. He will be there.'

Off they all went, Billy, Wilfred, and the young lady, who was just as excited as they were. Mr Lacy was in the shop, and when he was asked the question he nodded his head and said, yes.

'I sent home an engine and two carriages and a signal to the little boy belonging to Smith, the man who works here,' he said. 'That's how I passed on my good turn.'

'And *I'm* the little boy!' cried Billy. 'So my good turn worked all the way round back to me! How marvellous! I must set it going again, because I've still got to pass it on! What fun!'

So the next day he set another good turn going, and said: 'Pass it on, please!' Isn't it a fine idea! I'm going to do it too, aren't you?

The Boy Who Heard Too Much

There was once a boy called Harold, who had very sharp ears. He heard a great many things he shouldn't have heard, and he listened hard whenever he thought anyone was telling a secret.

He listened behind doors, too, which was a horrid thing to do. And sometimes he hid in the hedge and listened to what passers-by were saying, hoping that he would pick up a good secret.

His mother used to get angry with him.

'Something will happen to you one day!' she said. 'And then you'll be sorry you were such a nasty little listener!'

Something *did* happen as you will see! Poor silly Harold!

It happened one day that he was going through Windy Wood when he saw a bent old woman trotting along in front of him. It was Old Mother Two-Shoes, who was supposed to be as wise as anyone in the village. Where was she going?

Harold made up his mind to creep after her and see what she was going to do in the wood. Perhaps she was going to pick some strange herbs to make magic from. Perhaps she was going to dig up some hidden gold she kept in the wood!

But she didn't do either of those things. No, she went trotting on, humming a little song without much tune, until she came to a small tumble-down cottage in the heart of the wood.

Harold was surprised to see it there for he didn't know anyone lived in the wood. Aha, he was going to learn something about Mother Two-Shoes!

The old woman knocked at the door. Someone opened it and she went in. Harold saw the door shut, and he was disappointed. He couldn't hear much with the door shut! But the window was open – if he crept underneath that he *might* be able to hear what Mother Two-Shoes was talking about to the person who lived quite alone in the heart of the wood.

So he crept up to the window and bent down underneath. He pricked up his ears and listened hard.

'And how are you keeping, Goody?' he heard Mother Two-Shoes say. 'See, I've brought you a fine medicine, and a pound of my best butter.'

'I'm better, thank you,' he heard a quavering old voice say. 'Make some tea, Mother Two-Shoes. The kettle's on the boil.'

Mother Two-Shoes took down a teapot and poured some boiling water inside to warm it. Then, taking it to the window she flung the hot water out, meaning to put in the tea-leaves and make the tea.

And, of course, the hot water fell straight on to Harold, bending down under the window. It gave him such a shock that he yelled out:

'Oooooh!'

'My goodness, whatever's that!' said Mother Two-Shoes, startled. She leaned out of the window and saw Harold there, wiping his face and neck with a handkerchief and wishing to goodness he hadn't shouted out like that!

'Oh, so it's *you*, is it!' said Mother Two-Shoes, who knew very well what Harold was like. 'Listening again, I suppose! I've just come to visit my poor old friend, Goody, and *I've* no secrets for you to hear, you nasty little boy. Come here!'

Before Harold could run away she stretched out a long, skinny arm and caught hold of him by one of his ears. She pulled it hard – and then she pulled the other one. Harold squealed with pain, tore himself free and ran off.

'The more you peep,
The longer they'll keep!'

shouted Mother Two-Shoes after him.

Harold rubbed his smarting ears. How long they seemed! That horrid old woman had pulled them quite out of shape! He ran home and went to his bedroom. He looked in the glass on the wall – and then, oh dear me, what a terrible shock he got!

His ears had been pulled out as long as a hare's ears! They stood up above his head and turned this way and that just like a hare's. Harold looked most peculiar.

'Oh my goodness!' said Harold, staring at himself in horror. 'Look at that! Whatever am I to do?'

'Harold, Harold, tea-time!' called his mother from downstairs. Harold didn't answer. How could he go down to tea with ears like a hare?

'HAROLD!' shouted his mother. 'Do you hear me? Come down at once!'

Still Harold didn't answer. Tears came into his eyes, and he rubbed them away. His mother, cross and impatient, came running up the stairs. She flung open the door – and then stopped in the greatest surprise.

'Harold!' she said. 'What have you done with yourself? Why are you wearing those silly ears? Take them off and come down to tea at once.'

'I c-c-can't, Mother,' said Harold.

'Well, if you can't, I will!' said his mother, and pulled hard at his ears, thinking that it was a sort of ear-toy he was wearing to make himself look funny.

'Ow-ooh-ah!' yelled poor Harold – for, of course, the ears were really growing!

'My goodness!' said his mother, in alarm. 'Harold! Those are not really your ears, are they?'

'Yes, Mother,' sobbed Harold, and he told her all about Mother Two-Shoes and how she had punished him for listening.

'Well, didn't I always say something dreadful would happen to you one day?' said his mother. 'It's a nasty horrid habit, listening and prying round after other people. Now see what's happened! Whatever are you going to do?'

'I can wear a hat always,' said Harold, wiping his eyes.

'But the teacher won't let you wear it at

school,' said his mother.

'Perhaps she would if you wrote her a note and said there was something wrong with my ears so please would she let me keep my hat on,' said Harold.

His mother agreed to do that. So the next morning, wearing his biggest hat, Harold went to school with a note from his mother. The teacher read it, looked surprised, but told Harold he could keep his hat on as his mother wished it.

So he did, though the other children laughed at him very much. When the time came for play he went out with the others – and then he noticed that two boys were standing by themselves in a corner, whispering to one another. A secret! What could it be?

Harold went as near as he could and listened carefully. He could just hear what they were saying – his ears listened hard – and then a strange thing happened!

Something pushed his hat right off his head and it fell on the ground! Harold put up his hand – and found, to his horror, that his ears had grown twice as long, very suddenly, and had pushed his hat off his head!

The other children ran up and pointed at him.

'Long ears, long ears!' they cried. 'Donkey's ears for listening! Look how they've grown! Aha, Harold, listen some more and your ears will grow even longer! Long ears, long ears!'

Harold burst into tears and ran home. His mother was horrified when she found that his ears were now twice as long. She at once put on her bonnet and shawl and ran round to Mother Two-Shoes.

'Oh, please, good mother, take away my boy's long ears!' she begged. 'They are twice as long as they were, and I'm afraid they will grow even longer!'

'That's quite likely,' said Mother Two-Shoes. 'I'm sorry, Mrs Brown, but I can't cure Harold. Nobody can – except perhaps my cousin who is half a witch, and lives on the top of Hoo-Hoo Hill.'

'Oh, I'll send him there then,' said poor Mrs Brown, and she hurried home and told Harold to take his things and go to Dame Clip-Clop who lived on Hoo-Hoo Hill.

Harold didn't want to go at all, but he had to. He felt that he really couldn't live at home and have all the children coming pointing and shouting at him. It was too dreadful. So he packed a few things, said goodbye to his mother and went off to Dame Clip-Clop's.

Dame Clip-Clop was expecting him. She was a tall old lady, with bright, piercing eyes. She wore a big bonnet with white lace inside, and a red cloak that swirled round her as she tap-tapped quickly here and there with her stick.

'Oh, here you are,' she said, giving Harold a sharp look, and feeling his long ears with her horny hands. 'Dear, dear – never did I see such long ears on anyone! Well, they will be *very* useful to me!'

'How?' asked Harold.

'Speak up, speak up!' said Dame Clip-Clop. 'I'm very deaf indeed. Can't hear a word!'

And she certainly *was* deaf! Harold had to shout his loudest to make her hear, and sometimes he had to write down what he wanted to say on Dame Clip-Clop's big black slate.

Dame Clip-Clop kept Harold very busy indeed. She used him as her ears. All that she couldn't hear and wanted to hear she made him hear for her.

'Now listen, Harold,' she would say one morning. 'I want to know what the thrush is saying today. He has come to me with a message from a friend of mine. Go out into the garden and listen carefully, please. Write down the message you hear the thrush sing and tell me afterwards.'

Out Harold went. First of all he had to find the thrush because, shameful to say, although he knew what a thrush looked like, he had never bothered before to listen to its beautiful song and so, unless he saw the thrush first, he didn't know which of all the many bird-songs to listen to.

The thrush was sitting at the top of an ash tree. Its throat swelled as it sang. At first Harold couldn't make out at all what it was saying. He sat down on the grass and looked up at the thrush, listening hard. The sky was very blue, the sun was very warm.

'Blue, blue, blue!' sang the thrush. 'Do you see it, do you see it? Pretty, pretty! Look at your ears, look at your ears! Why did you do it, why did you do it?'

Harold went red. To think that even the thrushes in the garden noticed his long ears and sang about it! He went on listening, and soon, because the thrush had a very lovely voice, he couldn't help feeling happy to hear its song. He wrote down its song and took it to Dame Clip-Clop.

'The thrush does sing beautifully,' he said.

'Didn't you know that before?' said the old lady. 'Dear me, wherever were your ears?'

Another day she sent him to the waterfall and told him to bring back the tune it sang. He took his lunch with him for the way was long. He sat down by the silvery waterfall, ate his lunch and listened.

The water gurgled and bubbled, it had deep, bell-like notes, it had silvery ripples of tunes. Harold listened in delight and surprise. Whoever would have thought that water sang like that? He took out a little flute that Dame Clip-Clop had given him, and tried a little tune on it. The notes came bubbling out like the water.

All the afternoon Harold worked hard, trying to get the gurgling tune that the water sang. At last he had it and proudly went back to Dame Clip-Clop. He played her the liquid, silvery tune as loudly as he could, and she smiled, pleased.

'Yes, you have listened well,' she said. 'That is the tune I used to love when I could hear.'

'I didn't know water sang so beautifully,' said Harold.

'You didn't know much,' said Dame Clip-Clop. 'You just knew the things you shouldn't know – everybody else's business!'

One windy day Dame Clip-Clop told Harold to put on his coat and hat and go to the woods. 'The trees will have a message for me today,' she said. 'Go to the woods and find out what it is.'

Harold went, warmly wrapped up, for the wind was strong and cold. When he got to the woods he found a thick bush which sheltered him from the wind and sat down. 'This is a horrid, boring job!' he said to himself. 'It's cold, and who cares what the wind says in the trees!'

His big ears began to listen. The wind rushed through the wood. The leaves whispered loudly, saying: 'Sh! Sh! Sh!' The branches tossed and shouted for joy. The trees bent over sideways and roared to the gale that swept through them. Harold was surprised. Who would have thought that the wood could whisper, shout and roar like that? He listened carefully and soon made out the mad, exciting song that the trees sang to the wind. He wrote it down, and then, leaning back, he shut his eyes and listened again. It was grand.

Dame Clip-Clop read the song and said he had got the message very well.

'Do you know, I'd no idea the wind in the trees sounded so grand,' said Harold. 'It was wonderful.'

'Yes, ears are wonderful things when they are used right,' said the old dame. 'Tonight, when it is dark, go out into my garden and sit on the old seat. I want to know what goes on there when day is gone.'

So, half-frightened, Harold went out into the darkness that night. He sat down on the old seat and listened, his great ears pointing this way and that like a rabbit's.

'This is a silly thing to do,' thought Harold. 'I shall only be frightened by something. Besides, there's nothing to hear!'

'Too-whoo, too-whoo!' suddenly hooted an owl. Then, far away in the distance came an answering cry, 'Ooooo! Ooo-oo-oo-oo!'

The moon came slowly out from behind a cloud. Three little bats flew into the moonlight and Harold could hear their shrill, high, excited squeaks as they caught beetles in the air. Then, not far off in the hedge he heard a few happy squeals as a tiny fieldmouse hunted for food, talking to his small companion all the time.

The wind creaked in a big ash tree, and some small sparrows, roosting in the hedge nearby, awoke and chirruped in whispers before they went to sleep again. A hedgehog came shuffling across the grass and brushed against Harold's foot, giving a tiny grunt as it did so. Then a nightingale began to sing.

Harold stayed out in the night so long that Dame Clip-Clop had to fetch him in.

'Oh, why did you bring me in?' said the boy. 'It was lovely out there in the garden. You've no idea what I heard!'

'Oh, yes, I have,' said the old dame, smiling. 'But you shall tell me.'

Harold told her everything he had heard. 'You wouldn't believe the little friendly sounds that go on in the night,' he said, 'and oh, that nightingale! It didn't sound like a bird. It sounded like a fairy princess.'

'Well, now you'd better go to bed,' said Dame Clip-Clop.

The next night, just as Harold was going to sleep, he heard a sound a long way off. What was it? It sounded like some little animal in pain. It was a squeal. There! It came again! Harold jumped up, flung on his coat and trousers and ran downstairs.

'Where are you going?' called Dame Clip-Clop.

'I heard an animal squealing for help,' said Harold, and ran out into the night. He ran stumbling down the garden and out into the lane. He listened again. Yes, it came from the little wood down the hill. He ran on again, getting nearer and nearer.

The moon came out to help him. It shone down on a small rabbit, which had one of its feet caught in a trap. It was squealing pitifully. Harold forced open the trap and picked up the trembling creature. He put it under his coat and walked back to Dame Clip-Clop's.

He bathed the poor little paw and bound it up. The rabbit snuggled to him and looked at him gratefully out of big, soft eyes. Dame Clip-Clop watched.

'Have you ever heard a rabbit squealing in the night before?' she asked.

'I've never *noticed* it before,' said Harold, 'though I expect I've heard the noise many times.'

'I think you know now what things are right and good to listen to, don't you?' asked Dame Clip-Clop. 'Shall you ever waste your time prying and peeping and listening to other people's secrets again?'

'What, waste my hearing on things like that!' cried Harold. 'Why, there isn't enough time to go about hearing all the lovely things there are! No, I shall never make such a mistake again!'

'Then I think we will give your long ears to this little rabbit!' said Dame Clip-Clop, smiling. She stretched out her hands and pulled Harold's long ears gently from his head. They came away easily, leaving his own pink, rounded ears underneath. The old dame pressed the long ears on to the rabbit's furry head, and in a trice its smaller ears had vanished and it had fine, long ears instead.

'Now go, little beastie,' said Dame Clip-Clop, to the rabbit. 'You have long ears to hear enemies with. Use them well, and keep out of danger!'

The rabbit limped out of the door, turned to have a last look at the boy who had saved him and then disappeared. Harold went to a mirror and looked at himself in delight.

'Let your ears hear all the lovely songs and sounds of the world,' said the old dame, 'and let them hear, too, any calls for help, however faint. But close them to all secrets that are not yours, and to all things that are hateful or mean.'

'I will!' said Harold, and he meant it. He went home the next day and his mother was delighted to see he no longer had his long and pointed ears.

'Are your ears quite better now?' she asked, kissing him.

'Yes,' said Harold. 'They can only hear the right things now, Mother, and not the wrong things. I shall never grow long ears again.'

And you will be glad to hear that he never, never did.

The Skittle-policeman

Angela had a box of funny skittle-men. Each man was different. One was a clown with a pointed hat. One was a soldier in red. Another was a sailor in a sailor suit, and a fourth was a policeman in blue. There were nine altogether, and in the box were three balls, red, white, and blue.

Angela used to stand the skittles up in two rows and then she and Nanny used to throw the balls at them and see who could knock down the most. It was great fun.

One day the skittle that looked like a policeman was hit seven times in one morning, and the seventh time a dreadful thing happened. His wooden nose came off! Yes, it did, and it rolled over the floor into a corner. The policeman-skittle was shocked and sad. Fancy having no nose! How dreadful he would look!

When Angela picked him up she squealed in dismay. 'Oh, Nanny! He's lost his nose! I don't like him.'

'Don't be silly,' said Nanny. 'I'll find his nose and stick it on for you again. Then he'll be all right.'

But they couldn't find his nose, however hard they looked. Angela didn't like the policeman-skittle after that. She said he looked so horrid without a nose, and when Nanny had gone out of the room what do you think Angela did? She threw the skittle out of the window into the garden below! Wasn't it horrid of her?

Poor skittle! He fell into the wet grass and lay there, astonished and hurt. What was he going to do now!

All day long he lay there, and all day long it rained hard! When night came you wouldn't have known the skittle. All the paint had run off him, and he was just plain wood.

When the rain stopped and the moon shone out at night, the policeman-skittle sat up. He looked at himself. Goodness, what a sight he was! He felt his face. No nose! It was really dreadful. He wondered if he could find his nose if he went back to the nursery.

Somehow or other he climbed up the old apple tree by the wall and slipped in at the nursery window. The other toys were playing about on the floor very happily. When they saw the poor skittle-policeman with all his paint washed off him by the rain, they didn't know him.

'Who are you?' they shouted.

'I'm one of the skittle-men,' said the policeman, humbly. 'My nose was knocked off this morning and I've just come to see if I can find it.'

'How awful you look without a nose!' said the sailor doll, unkindly. 'And you've no paint at all.'

'I can't help it,' said the skittle, sadly. 'It isn't my fault. It's Angela's fault.'

'Well, we don't want you back here,' said the toys to the poor washed-out skittle. 'You look dreadful. Angela threw you away and you must stay away.'

'All right,' said the skittle, sighing. 'Just let me find my nose and I'll go. But I think you're very horrid and unkind.'

So they were, weren't they? Nobody helped the skittle to look for his nose, but he found it at last. He picked it up and went to the window.

'Goodbye,' he said. 'I'm sorry to leave you all.'

'Goodbye,' said the toys, and they turned their backs on him and began to play games again. The skittle slid down the apple tree and stood in the grass, wondering what to do.

He began to walk down the garden. He slipped under the hedge at the bottom and found himself in a field. He walked across it and came to a sloping hill-side.

The moon shone brightly. The skittle came to a little ring of toadstools, and then he heard a strange sound of grunting and panting. He looked to see what it was. To his great surprise he saw a small brownie tugging and pulling at the toadstools, trying his hardest to pull them up to carry away. But he couldn't drag the toadstools out of the ground, and at last he sat down on one, sighed heavily and said: 'I shall never do it. I shall NEVER do it!'

The skittle felt sorry for the little creature. He walked up to one of the toadstools and tugged. Plip! It came away from the ground at once. In fact it gave way so suddenly that the skittle sat down hard on the ground and said 'Oooh!' very loudly.

The brownie saw him and began to laugh. How he laughed! He laughed so much that the skittle began to laugh too.

'I say, I know I oughtn't to laugh at you when you were trying to help me,' said the brownie, stopping at last. 'But you looked so funny. Who are you?'

'I'm a skittle-policeman,' said the skittle. 'I've had my nose broken off, and Angela threw me out of the window because she didn't like me any more. Then the rain came and washed all my paint off me, so I haven't even a uniform on now. I'm afraid I look a dreadful creature.'

'You do look rather odd,' said the brownie, staring at him. 'But you can't help it. I say, aren't you strong? Could you help me to move these toadstools, do you think?'

'Of course,' said the skittle. 'But why do you want to move them? They look all right just here.'

'The silly things have grown in the wrong place,' said the brownie. 'They should have grown over there, where the magic bus stops – see, by that bush. They are seats for people waiting for the bus.'

'Oh,' said the skittle, looking in surprise at a bus that suddenly appeared round the bush. It wasn't much bigger than the toy bus in the nursery. It was full of mice, rabbits, and fairies. He stared and stared.

The bus drove off. The brownie began to tug hard at the toadstools again. 'Let me do it,' said the skittle, and he soon lifted two or three. The brownie carried them to the bus-stop and stood them there in a row. Presently little folk and three mice came along to wait for the bus. They were delighted to find the seats there and soon they were all full.

'It's very good of you to help me,' said the brownie, when they had taken up all the toadstools and moved them to their right places. 'I suppose I can't give you a cup of hot cocoa just to warm you up on this cold night?'

'Well, I'm quite warm,' said the skittle. 'But a cup of hot cocoa does sound very nice.'

'Come on, then,' said the brownie, and he took the skittle through a tiny door in the hill-side. Inside was a small and cosy room. A fire was burning at the end, and a kettle was singing on the hob. The brownie got out a cocoa tin and made some cocoa. Before long the skittle and the brownie were very friendly.

'It's a pity about your nose,' said the brownie. 'You would be nice-looking if you had a nose.'

'Well, I've got it here,' said the skittle. 'But what's the good of a nose in your pocket?'

'Oh, you've got it, have you!' said the brownie. 'Well, why not let me stick it on for you?'

'Oh, *could* you!' cried the skittle, delighted.

'Of course,' said the brownie. 'I can get some sticky glue from the buds of the chestnut tree, you know. The bees will go and collect enough for me. They are very clever at getting chestnut glue. Then I can stick your nose on for you.'

That night the skittle slept in the brownie's bed with the brownie. He was happy, warm, and comfortable. This was better than living in the nursery with unkind toys and a little girl who threw you out of the window because you had lost your nose.

In the morning the sun shone. The brownie went outside and made a strange humming sound. Soon twelve brown-and-gold bees came flying up to hear what the brownie had to say.

'Collect me some sticky glue from the chestnut buds,' he said. Off they flew. Soon they were back with the glue and they each put their sticky gift into a dish set ready for them. The brownie thanked them and went indoors. He heated the glue over the fire and then called the skittle to him. He took the little nose from him, smeared it with glue, and then stuck it firmly on the skittle's face. He stuck it on just a little bit crooked, but it didn't matter – it just made the skittle look comical and jolly.

'Ooh!' said the skittle, for the glue was hot. He stood still, quite brave, and in a few minutes there was his nose, firmly on his face again. How pleased he was!

'Many, many thanks,' he said, looking at himself in a looking-glass. 'That's fine! If only I could get myself a new coat of paint I should look just as grand as ever I did!'

'Well, perhaps we can manage that too,' said the brownie, at once. 'I know the elf who paints the bluebells in the spring, and if you don't mind rather a pale-blue for your uniform, I'm sure she would come and do it for you.

The skittle-policeman didn't know what to say, he was so pleased and grateful. Tears came into his eyes, and ran down his nose.

'I say, don't do that!' said the brownie, in alarm. 'Your nose is only just stuck, you know! If you cry tears, it might come unstuck.'

The skittle hurriedly dried his tears and smiled. 'You are very good and kind to me,' he said. 'I would simply *love* a bluebell-coloured uniform.'

So the next thing that happened was that they went to call on the elf who always painted the bluebells in May. She was pleased to see them and at once agreed to give the skittle a fine new

blue uniform. She set to work that same day and you should have seen the policeman-skittle when she had finished. He looked simply beautiful.

'You look grand enough to go to Toytown and be the policeman there!' said the elf, looking at the skittle, very pleased with her painting. 'The policeman there is old, and doesn't know how to deal with all the new traffic that's come in the last few years. You know, buses, trams, trains, motor-cars, and all that. Toytown used to be a peaceful sort of spot, but now it's all different.'

The skittle-policeman listened, his eyes shining. How he had longed to be a real policeman and stand in the road with his hand out! But he had never been anything but a skittle, made to be knocked down and set up again.

'Oh,' he said. 'Oh! If only they'd let me try to do some proper policeman's work in Toytown! How hard I would work! How careful I would be! I would see that no accident happened and that everything went at the right speed.'

The brownie and the elf stared at one another in excitement. 'Come along!' they suddenly cried to the surprised skittle. 'Come along!

We'll get you the job! Oh, how pleased Toytown will be to have a new policeman!'

Soon the skittle found himself being dragged along to the bus at the corner. They all got in and in ten minutes' time they arrived at Toytown. The skittle felt quite at home when he saw teddy bears, dolls, and toy dogs walking about the streets. Everyone stared at him in admiration, for he really did look smart in his beautiful pale-blue uniform.

Well, he got the job, of course. The old policeman was only too glad to give it up.

The skittle walked proudly into the middle of the town, where the traffic was thickest, and five roads met. He held up his arm. Everything stopped at once. That was a proud moment for the skittle. He waved his hand. The cars and buses chugged onwards again.

Everyone came to look at the new policeman.

'What a beautiful uniform he has!' they cried. 'What a lovely nose, just the weeniest bit crooked! Most unusual! How well he guides the traffic! He is a fine policeman, one to be proud of.'

What do you think happened one day? A big motor-car came up, driven by a sailor doll. At the back were crowded a pack of skittle-men, two dolls, and a teddy bear – and they were all from Angela's nursery, where the skittle-policeman had once lived!

'Honk, honk!' said the car, impatiently, for the sailor doll was in a hurry. The skittle-policeman knew that honk, and he looked round sharply. Ah, it was the toys he had once known! They were going too fast. He put up his hand to stop them. The sailor doll stopped, frowning. He was afraid of this policeman in his beautiful uniform.

Suddenly the teddy bear gave a squeal.

'It's the policeman-skittle from the nursery, the one whose nose came off! Just look at him! Oooooh!'

The policeman turned round and looked at the toys. He didn't smile. He didn't blink an eye. He just looked at them very sternly.

The toys in the car went pale. They felt uncomfortable. They remembered how unkind they had been. The little doll burst into tears. The policeman-skittle said nothing at all. He waited until the road was clear and then he waved on the motor-car. The sailor doll was so nervous that he put on the brake instead of starting the car and the toys nearly fell out with the jerk.

'Come along, now, come along, now,' said the skittle in his deepest voice. 'Don't hold up the traffic.'

The car at last went on. All the skittles stared back at the policeman in fear and admiration. What a grand fellow he was, to be sure! How sorry they were they had been unkind! Dear, dear, dear, what a mistake they had made! How they wished they were friends with him now!

But it was no use wishing. Once a chance of kindness is lost, it is gone for ever. The toys were very silent that day, and all of them were secretly making up their minds to be nicer in future.

As for the skittle-policeman, how he laughed when he told the brownie and the elf about the toys that night.

'You should have taken them all to prison,' said the brownie, indignantly, for he was very fond of his skittle friend now.

'Oh, no,' said the policeman. 'I just looked at them like this – and they felt dreadful, I know they did!'

'You are a kind and clever fellow,' said the elf, and she hugged the skittle. 'Let's get married and then I can paint you a new uniform every year when I do the bluebells.'

So they are married now, and very happy. And every day the skittle can be seen in Toytown, right in the middle of the street, stopping the traffic and waving it on just like any policeman in your own town. Wouldn't you like to see him? I would!

Tick Tock's Tea-party

Tick-Tock the brownie lived with the enchanter Wind-Whistle, and kept his house neat and tidy for him. He cooked his meals, washed his clothes, and sometimes he helped Wind-Whistle with his spells. He was hard at work all day long, but he was very happy.

One afternoon there came a knock at the door and Tick-Tock went to open it. Outside stood the Princess of the Blue Hills and two of her court, come to visit the enchanter and take his advice.

It was just tea-time and Tick-Tock knew they would all stay to tea – and oh, dear me – there were no cakes at all, hardly any jam, and just a pinch of tea!

'Pray come inside!' said Tick-Tock, bowing low, for he knew his manners very well. The Princess came in, smelling very sweet and looking very lovely. Tick-Tock gave her and the ladies-in-waiting some chairs in the drawing-room and went to tell Wind-Whistle of his royal visitor. All the time he was worrying about tea. What should he do for cakes and jam? You couldn't give royal princesses plain bread and butter – and goodness gracious, there was hardly any butter either! It was very worrying.

Wind-Whistle was pleased to hear of his royal visitor. He put on his best cloak at once and said to Tick-Tock: 'Get tea ready. Lay it nicely.'

'Oh, your highness, isn't it dreadful, there are no cakes, just a pinch of tea, hardly any jam, and not much butter!' said poor Tick-Tock.

'Well, go to the shops and get some,' said the enchanter snappily.

'But they're shut this afternoon,' said Tick-Tock. 'It's early closing day!'

'Dear, dear, so it is,' said the enchanter. 'Well, never mind. Now listen carefully, Tick-Tock. Lay the table as usual, but place the butter-dish, the jam-dish, and cake-dishes empty on the table – empty, do you hear? Put no tea in the teapot, but fill it with boiling water. I have a mind to do a little magic for the Princess, and at the same time provide a good tea for her.'

Tick-Tock listened open-mouthed. How exciting!

He hurried to do what he was told. He laid

the table, put out empty butter, jam, and cake-dishes, and filled the teapot with boiling water. Then he told the enchanter that everything was ready.

Wind-Whistle led the Princess and her ladies into the room where the tea was laid and bade them be seated. They were surprised to see nothing to eat.

'Madam, do you like Indian or China tea?' began the enchanter, holding up the tea-pot. Then he caught sight of the brownie Tick-Tock peeping in at the door to watch everything.

'Go to the kitchen!' he ordered. 'And shut this door, Tick-Tock.'

Poor Tick-Tock! He had so badly wanted to see everything. He shut the door and went to the kitchen – but in half a minute he was back again, peeping through the keyhole and listening to what the enchanter was saying!

'I'll have China tea,' said the Princess.

'China tea, pour forth!' commanded the enchanter, and the Princess gave a scream of delight, for pale China tea poured from the teapot into her cup.

'I'd like Indian tea,' said each of her ladies, and when Wind-Whistle said: 'Indian tea, pour forth!' at once dark Indian tea poured into their cups.

'What sort of jam do you like?' asked Wind-Whistle.

'Strawberry, please,' answered his three royal visitors.

'Strawberry jam, appear in the dish!' cried Wind-Whistle. Immediately a great heap of delicious jam appeared.

'And what cakes do you prefer?' asked the enchanter.

'Chocolate cakes for me!' cried the Princess in excitement.

'Cherry buns for me!' said the first lady.

'And ginger fingers for me!' begged the second lady.

'Chocolate cakes, appear!' commanded the enchanter, tapping a dish. 'Cherry buns, come forth, ginger fingers, appear!'

Three dishes were suddenly full of the most delicious-looking cakes, and the ladies cried out in delight. Then the enchanter struck the butter-dish.

'Now, butter, where are you?' he cried. Golden butter at once gleamed in the dish. It was marvellous. Outside the door Tick-Tock listened to all this, and tried to see through the keyhole what was happening. It was most exciting.

After tea Wind-Whistle called Tick-Tock to him.

'I'm going to the Blue Hills with the Princess and her ladies,' he said. 'She needs my help. Look after my house and see that nothing goes wrong. And don't meddle with any magic or you will be sorry!'

By six o'clock Wind-Whistle and the ladies were gone and Tick-Tock was left alone. He finished up the cakes that were left from tea and enjoyed them very much. They were much nicer than any that were sold in the shops.

It was whilst he was eating the cakes that the naughty idea came to him. He clapped his hands for joy and danced round the kitchen.

'Why shouldn't I give a tea-party and make all the cakes and things appear!' he shouted. 'I can wear the enchanter's magic cloak, and then all the things I say will come true too. Oh, how lovely! Won't I make everyone stare! My friends will think *I'm* an enchanter.'

He sat down at once and wrote six notes to his friends. One went to Big-Eyes, one to Little-Feet, another to Pippity, the fourth to Gobo, and the last two to Tubby and Roundy the two fat brownies.

'Please come to a Magic Tea-Party,' he wrote to each of them. Then he licked up the envelopes and posted the letters. How excited he felt!

He had asked his friends for the next day. So he was very busy in the morning making the house tidy and putting fresh flowers on the tea-table. Then after his dinner he washed himself, did his hair nicely, laid the tea-table with empty plates and dishes, and at last went to put on the enchanter's magic cloak. It was embroidered with suns and moons and shone very brightly.

Tick-Tock walked about in front of the looking-glass in Wind-Whistle's bedroom and thought he looked really very grand.

'Won't I surprise everyone this afternoon!' he chuckled to himself. 'Dear me! There's the clock striking half-past three! I must put the kettle on for tea.'

He ran downstairs, nearly tripping over the cloak he wore, for it was much too big for him. He put the kettle on, and waited for his friends.

They all came together, looking very smart in their best clothes. They were most excited and crowded round Tick-Tock, asking him what a Magic Tea-Party was.

'Wait and see, wait and see!' said Tick-Tock, laughing.

He led them into the dining-room, where tea was laid – but when they saw the empty dishes their faces grew long. Wasn't there going to be anything to eat?

'Wait and see, wait and see!' laughed Tick-Tock, again, running into the kitchen to fetch the kettle, which was now boiling.

His guests sat down round the table, and waited. Tick-Tock came back with the kettle. He was going to do better than the enchanter – he was going to make the cakes, jam, butter, and tea all appear at once!

'What sort of cakes and jam do you like?' he asked his guests. They all called out together.

'Gooseberry jam! Chocolate roll! Coconut buns! Cherry cake! Plum jam! Marmalade! Sponge fingers!'

'Right!' said Tick-Tock. He picked up the teapot, which he had filled with nothing but hot water, and then cried out loudly: 'Tea, pour forth! Butter, appear! Gooseberry jam, plum jam, marmalade, where are you? Chocolate roll, coconut buns, cherry cake, sponge fingers, come forth!'

Then, to the enormous surprise of all his

friends, the teapot poured tea into their cups, one after another, jam and marmalade began to come into the dishes, butter heaped itself up in another dish, and cakes fell into a pile on the rest of the dishes. It was perfectly marvellous!

'Wonderful!' cried Gobo.

'How do you do it!' shouted Tubby and Roundy.

'Goodness gracious!' cried the others.

'It's easy!' said Tick-Tock, pouring out his cup of tea last of all. 'I'm quite a good magician, you know. I'm sure I could teach Wind-Whistle a lot.'

A puzzled look came over the faces of the six guests as they watched the jam, butter, and cakes appearing in the dishes. They had been appearing for quite a while now, and the dishes were much too full. In fact the gooseberry jam was spilling on to the cloth.

'You ought to have put out bigger dishes,' said Tubby to Tick-Tock. 'Look, they aren't big enough for all the cakes and things.'

But Tick-Tock was also feeling puzzled about something and didn't hear what Tubby said. The teapot had filled his cup, but when he set it down on the teapot stand, it didn't stay there. No, it hopped up into the air all by itself and began to pour tea into the milk-jug! It was most peculiar. Tick-Tock took hold of it and put it back on the tray. But as soon as he let go, up hopped the teapot into the air again and poured a stream of tea into the sugar-basin. It was most annoying.

'I say, Tick-Tock, the dishes aren't *big* enough, I tell you!' said Tubby, as he and the others watched the cakes spilling all over the table. 'Shall we get some more?'

'No, just help yourselves and eat as much as you want to,' said Tick-Tock, still busy with the obstinate teapot. 'If you eat up the cakes there will soon be room for them on the dishes.'

So the guests began eating – but, dear me, they couldn't eat nearly as fast as those cakes, jams, and butter appeared! Soon the tablecloth was in a dreadful mess, for the jam slid over the edge of the pot and dripped on to the table, and the butter flopped down too, while the marmalade was in big blobs all round its dish. The cakes no longer fell on the dishes as they appeared out of the air, but bounced straight on to the table, scattering crumbs all over the place.

The guests were rather frightened, especially when they saw what trouble the teapot was giving poor Tick-Tock. But they said no more.

They ate steadily, though nothing really tasted very nice. Poor Tick-Tock could eat nothing for all the time he was trying to stop the teapot from pouring tea here, there, and everywhere.

At last it tore itself away from the frightened brownie and poured some tea down Gobo's neck!

'Ow!' squealed Gobo, jumping up in fright as the hot tea dripped down his collar. 'Ow! Ooh! It's burnt me!'

He wiped the tea away with his handkerchief and began to cry.

'Hoo, hoohoo! I'm going home! This isn't a nice tea-party.'

He ran out of the door and slammed it. The others looked at one another. The teapot moved towards Tubby, but he jumped out of the way.

'Good-bye, Tick-Tock,' he said. 'I must get home. I've some work to do.'

'I must go with him,' said Roundy, and the two brownies ran off in a hurry.

It wasn't long before the other guests went too. The magic was frightening them. It was all very well to have as many cakes as you wanted, but to see hundreds dropping on to the table was very queer. They felt sure something had gone wrong.

Tick-Tock was very unhappy and rather frightened. What had happened? Hadn't he done the magic just the same as Wind-Whistle? Why wouldn't everything stop appearing? Why didn't that horrid teapot stop pouring?

Tick-Tock looked round the table in despair. What a mess! Look at all the jam and marmalade! Look at those cakes, not even bothering to fall on the dishes any more! Look at the butter all over the place! And look at that perfect nuisance of a teapot pouring tea on the carpet now! Whatever was he to do?

Poor Tick-Tock! He couldn't do anything. He had started a magic that he couldn't stop. The teapot suddenly stopped pouring tea on the carpet and playfully poured some on Tick-Tock's beautiful cloak. He cried out in dismay.

'Oh! Look what you've done to the enchanter's best cloak! Oh, what a mess! Whatever will he say? Oh, my goodness me, I must go and sponge off the tea at once!'

Tick-Tock rushed upstairs to the bathroom. He took a sponge and began to sponge the tea-stain on the cloak. He was dreadfully afraid the enchanter would see it, and what would he say then? Oh, dear, dear, why ever had Tick-Tock meddled with magic when he had been told not to?

It took a long time to get the tea-stain out of the cloak, but at last it was done. Tick-Tock hung the cloak over a chair to dry and was just going downstairs when he heard someone shouting from outside the house. He stuck his head out of the window to see what the matter was.

Out of doors stood Gobo, and he was shouting at the top of his voice.

'Hi, Tick-Tock! Are you all right? There are a lot of funny things happening down here! Look!'

Tick-Tock looked – and out of the front door he saw a stream of tea flowing! Yes, really, it was running down the path! Mixed with it was butter, jam, marmalade, and cakes of all kinds, bobbing up and down in the stream.

'Oooooh!' screamed Tick-Tock, and ran downstairs in a hurry. Well! I couldn't tell you what the dining-room looked like. It was a foot deep in tea, to begin with, for the teapot was still pouring away merrily. And then the cakes! Well, there were hundreds and hundreds of them. The jam and marmalade and butter were all mixed up together, and still more and more things were dropping down into the room

Tick-Tock waded in. The teapot at once

poured some tea on his nose and he gave a cry of pain, for it was hot. Whatever was he to do? This was dreadful.

'Can't you stop the things coming and coming and coming?' shouted Gobo, who was really very sorry for his friend. 'You made them start.'

'I know,' sobbed Tick-Tock. 'But I thought they would stop by themselves and they haven't. If only Wind-Whistle was here!'

Then Gobo gave a shout and pointed up the street. 'Here he comes!' he cried. 'He's come home sooner than you thought!'

So he had. Poor Tick-Tock! He didn't know whether to be glad or sorry. Wind-Whistle strode up the road and when he came to his house and saw the stream of tea pouring out, mixed with jam and cakes, he was most astonished. He stared at it in amazement, whilst poor Tick-Tock tried to stammer all about it.

'What! You dared to meddle with magic when I told you not to!' shouted the enchanter in anger. 'You wore my magic cloak! How dare you?'

'Oh, please, your highness, forgive me!' wept the brownie, as white as a sheet. 'I just thought I would give a tea-party like you did. It looked so easy. But nothing would stop. It just went on and on. The teapot is still pouring in the dining-room.'

The enchanter waded through the stream of tea and looked in at the dining-room door. What a dreadful sight! He frowned in anger. Then he clapped his hands sharply three times and said: 'Illa rimmytooma lippitty crim!' These words were so magic that Tick-Tock trembled to hear them. But at the sound of them the teapot at once stopped its pouring and put itself in the sink to be washed up. The cakes stopped falling from the air, and so did the jam, marmalade, and butter.

But the dreadful mess remained. Tick-Tock looked at it in despair.

'Aren't you going to make all this mess go too?' he asked his master.

'No, *you're* going to make that go!' said Wind-Whistle, sternly. 'Get brushes, cloths, soap and water, Tick-Tock, and clear it up. It will keep you busy.'

Tick-Tock went away howling. The mess would take him days to clear up. But it was his own fault, he shouldn't have meddled with magic. He never would again, never!

Wind-Whistle forgave Tick-Tock, when the house was clean and tidy again. But when he wants to tease the little brownie, he says: 'Would you like another tea-party, Tick-Tock, some day?'

But Tick-Tock shakes his head and cries: 'No, no, no. Never again!'

The Runaway Donkey

There was once a gnome who owned a fat grey donkey. The donkey was called Kick-up, because when he was angry he kicked up his hind legs. He had a good home with his master, the gnome Twiddle, and although Twiddle was very fond of the donkey, and did all he could to make him comfortable, Kick-up was always complaining.

Once Twiddle bought a dog, but the donkey made such a fuss that he had to sell it again.

'How can I sleep when that dog barks all night?' complained Kick-up. 'I won't work for you, Twiddle, if you keep him as well as me.'

Then Twiddle tried keeping hens, for he was very fond of boiled eggs. Kick-up kicked up his heels in a fury, and sent a basket of eggs, which Twiddle was carrying carefully, right up into the air – and, of course, all the eggs broke.

'Well, why do you keep those nasty, clucking creatures?' cried Kick-up in a rage. 'As soon as I lie down for a snooze in my field those hens lay eggs and start the most terrible cackling I ever heard. Is it such a grand thing to lay an egg? No, it is not. Even snails lay eggs.'

'Don't worry yourself,' said Twiddle, gently, for he was a good-tempered gnome. 'If the hens disturb you, Kick-up, they shall go. I will give them to my next-door neighbour. You know that I am very fond of you, and I want you to be happy.'

One day Twiddle dug up a great many potatoes and thought he would take them to market to sell. He had far more than he could eat, and he thought it would be nice to sell some, and with the money buy some paint to make Kick-up's stable smart.

So he spoke to Kick-up and told him that he must take him to market the next day, carrying a load of potatoes.

Now Kick-up had grown fat and lazy. He had planned to snooze in the hot sunshine all the next day, and he was cross to hear that he was to go all the way to market, carrying a heavy load.

'Master, you work me too hard,' he complained. 'It is too hot to carry loads to market. I shall get sunstroke and then you will be sorry.'

'Then I will get you a sun-hat today,' said Twiddle. 'I shouldn't like you to get sunstroke, Kick-up, because I am really very fond of you. But you MUST go to market with me tomorrow. I cannot possibly carry the potatoes myself.'

'I tell you it is too hot to go to market,' said the donkey, sulkily. 'If you treat me like this, I shall run away. As for a sun-hat, I don't want one. I should look silly wearing a hat.'

But Twiddle was so afraid that his precious donkey *would* get sunstroke, for it was certainly very hot, that he went off to buy a large straw sun-hat for him, with two holes for his ears, and a large pink rose in front, to make the hat pretty. When he got back he slipped it over Kick-up's head, and tied the ribbon firmly under his chin.

'You look very nice,' said Twiddle, admiringly. Kick-up jumped up in a temper and ran to the pond. He looked at himself and then flew into a dreadful rage.

'I look foolish, stupid, ridiculous, and a perfect silly!' he shouted in a rage. 'Take the hat off at once, Twiddle.'

'Who is master, you or I?' said Twiddle, quite firmly, for once.

'I shall run away if you don't take off this hat!'

cried the donkey. At that the gnome turned his back on him and walked away, hoping that Kick-up would be in a better temper by the next day.

But do you know, when Twiddle went to Kick-up's stable the next morning, the door was open and Kick-up was not there! He had gone, quite gone.

Twiddle stared in the greatest surprise. Then he looked all round the fields – no little fat donkey was anywhere to be seen. It was terrible. Kick-up had kept his word, and had run away!

Twiddle's eyes filled with tears. He had had the donkey for ten years, and had cared for him and loved him very much. He would miss him dreadfully, even though the little donkey had been so bad-tempered.

'I must see if I can find him,' thought the gnome, and he set off for his friends' houses.

'Have you seen a fat, grey donkey wearing a sun-hat?' he asked Gobbo, who was feeding his hens in the back garden. 'He's run away.'

'Good riddance too!' said Gobbo, at once. 'Let's hope he stays away.'

'But I'm lonely without him,' said Twiddle.

'Poor old Twiddle,' said Gobbo. 'It's a shame. Look, please will you accept three white hens from me for a present? They will lay you lovely eggs for breakfast, and now that Kick-up is gone there is no one to grumble about their cackling.'

'Oh, thank you!' cried Twiddle, pleased. 'I shall love to have eggs for breakfast tomorrow.'

So he took the hens home in delight and put them into the hen-run. Then off he went to his friend Tiralee, who lived at the other end of the village.

'Have you seen my fat, grey donkey?' he asked. 'He's run away, and he's wearing a sun-hat.'

'No, I haven't seen him, and I don't want to,' said Tiralee. 'Horrid thing, he was, with his bad temper and rude ways. You are well rid of him.'

'But I'm lonely without him,' said Twiddle.

'Poor old Twiddle,' said Tiralee, who was very fond of his gentle friend. 'Look here, old man, I've got three beautiful puppies here. I'd like to give you one of them to keep you company. He'll grow up into a lovely dog, and be very fond of you.'

'Oh, thank you,' said Twiddle, gratefully. He took the puppy home and called him Tinker, which the puppy thought was a lovely name.

Kick-up hadn't come back, so off went Twiddle to the next village, to call on his friends there. He knocked at Tiptoes' door, and she opened it.

'Have you seen a fat, grey donkey wearing a sun-hat?' asked Twiddle. 'He's run away from me.'

'Well, don't have him back,' said Tiptoes, at once. 'You're well off without him, the bad-tempered creature!'

'But I'm lonely without him,' said Twiddle, mournfully. Then Tiptoes was sorry for the little gnome.

'What you want is a cat sitting by your fireside!' she said. 'Look, here is a little black kitten for you; it will bring you luck!'

Twiddle was delighted with the cuddly black kitten. He put it under his coat and then went to call on Too-tall, next door.

'Have you seen a fat, grey donkey wearing a sun-hat?' he asked Too-tall. 'He's run away.'

'*That's* a blessing!' said Too-tall, at once. 'I never did like that horrid donkey of yours.'

'Yes, but I'm lonely without him,' said Twiddle.

'Poor old Twiddle!' cried Too-tall. 'I'm sorry for you. Wait a minute. I've two tame pigeons you would simply love. They say "Coo-rco" all day and are fine company. I'll give you them.

They will perch on your hat all the way home, so you won't have any trouble with them!'

Twiddle was delighted with the pretty white pigeons. They perched on his hat at once and were quite at home there, pecking Twiddle's big ears lovingly every now and again.

Last of all Twiddle called on his friend Very-Rich, and knocked at his door. Very-Rich was pleased to see him and shook hands in delight.

'Have you seen a fat, grey donkey wearing a sun-hat?' asked Twiddle. 'He's run away.'

'Well, you can thank your lucky stars that he's gone, the wretched thing!' said Very-Rich, who had once been kicked by Kick-up, and had never forgotten it.

'But I'm lonely without him,' said Twiddle, 'and also, it's very, very awkward, because I've a load of potatoes to take to market and I've no donkey to take them now.'

'Well, well, well!' said his friend, scratching his head and thinking hard. 'Let me see. How would you like me to give you my old pony? I don't need her any more, and she would love to come and live with you. She can carry heavy loads and doesn't mind working at all.'

'Dear me, no, I couldn't take a present like that!' said Twiddle.

'Dear me, yes, you could!' laughed Very-Rich, and he went to fetch the pony. It ran up to Twiddle and nuzzled its nose into his hand. He was so pleased.

'Well, I *would* love to have this pony!' he said. 'Thank you very much. I'll treat her very well.'

'I know you will,' said Very-Rich.

Twiddle climbed up on the pony's back and jogged happily home, with the kitten under his coat, and the two pigeons on his head. What a lot of good friends he had! He certainly wouldn't be lonely now that he had so many animals and birds of his own. Three white hens, a nice puppy-dog, a kitten, two pigeons, and a pony! How lucky he was!

He put the pony into the donkey's stable and told the pigeons they might live there too, and pick up any corn they wished. The puppy he put in a nice little kennel, and the kitten he said might live by the fireside. The hens were very happy in their run.

For a whole week Twiddle and his new friends lived happily together. The pony took him to market and never complained at all. The dog guarded him each night, and always went with him for walks. The kitten sat on his knee and purred lovely things to him. The hens laid him three eggs every day, and the pigeons called 'coo-roo' whenever they saw him, and flew down to his shoulders. He was very happy.

Then one night, when Twiddle was fast asleep in bed, the fat, grey donkey came back! He had tried first one master and then another, he had been disobedient and bad-tempered, and he had been beaten and half-starved. He was sorry he had ever left kind Twiddle.

'He'll be glad to see me back,' thought the donkey, as he trotted homewards. 'He'll have been very lonely without me. He'll treat me better than ever now!'

It was dark when the donkey reached home.

He trotted into the yard and immediately the puppy-dog in the kennel began to bark and flew at him. Snap! He was bitten in the leg and he brayed with pain!

He ran to his stable, but the door was shut. He kicked it open and went inside. But someone else was there – the little pony! He kicked out with his hind feet and the donkey was struck smartly on the nose – biff! Then the pigeons flew down from the rafters and cried 'coo-roo' angrily at him, and pecked the tips of his ears!

Poor Kick-up! How frightened he was! This was a dreadful home-coming! He left the stable and went to the house, but on the way he woke up the hens who all started to cackle at once: 'kuk-kuk-kuk-kuk-kuk-kuk, a robber, kuk-kuk-kuk-kuk-kuk, a robber!'

Kick-up pushed open the kitchen door, which was never locked. He ran into the kitchen, anxious to get away from all the frightening things in the yard – but the kitten, who was sitting by the fire, flew at him in a rage, dug all her twenty claws into his legs, and spat at him so fiercely that he backed into the kitchen table in fright and over it went!

That woke up Twiddle. Wondering whatever was the matter, he lit his candle and went downstairs. As soon as the donkey saw him, he cried: 'Twiddle, what are all these things you have, that bite, kick, and scratch? Order them away at once! I have come home to keep you company again, because I was sorry to think of you sitting here lonely and sad without me.'

'Dear me, but I'm not at all lonely or sad,' said Twiddle, sharply. 'I have plenty of good company and jolly friends. What have you come back for? I don't want you! You always were a bad-tempered, disobedient, selfish animal, and I don't know how I put up with you. Be off with you! There's no room for you here!'

Kick-up was so surprised that he stood staring at his master, and didn't say a word.

'Go away, I tell you!' said Twiddle, angrily. 'What do you mean by disturbing us at this time of night? If you want to see me in the morning, you may come humbly to me and ask my pardon. I don't want to see you any more tonight.'

The donkey ran out of the kitchen and went into the field. It was wet and cold, but he did not dare to go to his stable again. He lay in the field all night, grieving and sighing. In the morning he went to Twiddle again.

'Master,' he said, hanging his head, 'forgive me. Take me back. Send away these horrid creatures and let me work for you as before. I will be a good donkey to you.'

'Stuff and nonsense,' said Twiddle, patting the puppy and stroking the purring kitten. 'I don't want you any more. If you like to live in the field next door and earn your keep by fetching and carrying for me, you can do so. But I don't want you to. I've quite enough animals here already.'

Kick-up had to live in the field. He had to work hard. The puppy barked at him. The kitten spat at him. The hens cackled loudly whenever he passed. The pigeons pecked his nose when they could. The pony stood ready to kick; so he wasn't very happy.

But he is learning his lesson. He doesn't complain now. He works hard. He is humble and quiet. Twiddle watches him out of the corner of his eye, because, you know, he really is fond of that silly grey donkey. So I expect he will forgive him one day and take him back – but you may be sure he will still keep his other friends. Ah, it was a good day for him when Kick-up ran away, wasn't it!

The Surprise Party

There was once a brown teddy bear who was always miserable. You should have seen him! He went about with a long face, his whiskers drooping and his ears down. Nobody knew what was the matter with him, they just knew that he was miserable, and that it didn't seem to be any good to try to cheer him up.

As for the teddy bear himself, he was a foolish fellow. He thought that nobody liked him or wanted him. When he saw the other toys laughing and joking together, giving each other presents, and helping one another, he pulled a longer face than ever. He thought it was too bad that they left him out of everything.

And the toys thought that it was too bad that he wouldn't join in anything – so you see things got worse and worse, and soon the teddy bear went and moped in a corner all day and wouldn't even answer when he was spoken to.

The toys laughed about it at first – and then, because they were kind-hearted, they began to worry about the teddy bear. They sent to the pixie who lived in the pansy bed under the nursery window and asked him for his advice. He was old and very wise.

He peeped in at the window and saw the brown bear moping in a corner, looking very lonely and miserable. He shook his head and thought for a long while.

'I'll tell you the best medicine for him,' he said at last. 'Give him a great big surprise! That's the best cure for anyone who's moping.'

'What sort of surprise?' asked the French doll.

'Oh, any kind, so long as it's nice,' said the pixie. 'That ought to cure him. Don't let him guess what we're doing, though, or that will spoil it.'

Well, the toys sat in a corner together and talked about it. What kind of surprise could they give the teddy bear? They really couldn't think of anything!

Then the yellow duck suddenly thought of something. 'Why,' she said, flapping her plush wings in delight, 'I know! It's the teddy bear's birthday on Saturday. He came from the same shop as I did, and I quite well remember him telling me one day when his birthday was.

Couldn't we give him a birthday party? That would be a wonderful surprise!'

All the toys thought the duck's plan was a very good one. So they began to think what they should do.

'I will make the teddy bear a fine blue sash,' said the French doll, who was very clever with her fingers. 'He will like that to wear at his party.'

'And I will make some chocolate buns on the little stove in the doll's house,' said the sailor doll, who was really a very good cook.

'I'll make some toffee!' cried the clockwork mouse.

'Sh!' said everyone. 'The teddy bear will hear you! Remember, it must all be a great surprise!'

The teddy bear heard all the toys whispering together in the corner, and he felt more out of things than ever. What were they whispering about now?

'I expect they are saying horrid things about me!' said the bear sulkily. 'Oh, dear, how I wish I didn't live in this horrid nursery, with all these horrid toys always whispering horrid things about me. I've a good mind to run away!'

The toys went on with their plans for the party. They decided to build a big house of the pink and blue toy bricks, and to hold the party there. Besides the chocolate buns there should be ginger fingers and sugar biscuits. The pixie promised to bring them some honey lemonade to drink. There were plenty of cups, saucers and plates in the dolls' tea-set for the toys to use. What fun it would be!

They would have games afterwards, and the teddy bear should choose them. The clockwork train promised that if it were wound up it would give the bear six rides round the nursery, which was really a very great treat indeed, for usually the toy train was lazy and wouldn't give a ride to anyone at all!

Then there were presents for the bear. There was a fine walking-stick. It was really a pencil with a curved end like a handle, and it belonged to the children whose nursery the toys lived in. But they had thrown the pencil away because it wouldn't write properly. The toys found it and thought it would make a fine walking-stick. So they polished it up and made it shine beautifully.

Then there was a little red and yellow brooch that had come out of a Christmas cracker. It was very pretty and the toys felt sure the bear would like it. There was also a pair of small blue shoes, too large for the smallest doll and too small for the other dolls. They would fit the teddy bear very well, the toys thought.

Nicest of all there was a wonderful little chair, made by the pixie outside, out of bent hazel and willow twigs woven together. That was really a fine surprise.

All the toys were to be in their best clothes. Those that hadn't best clothes, or no clothes at all were to wash themselves well and brush their fur or hair. The party was to begin at four o'clock with a song made up by the sailor doll especially for the teddy bear.

The toys were more excited that week than they had ever been before. What whispering there was! What planning! What laughing and joking!

The teddy bear couldn't for the life of him make out what was happening. He tried to listen to the whispering but all he heard was 'the party'. Then he was more unhappy than ever because he felt sure the toys were going to have a party without him.

'They don't want me,' said the poor foolish bear. 'They're going to have a party and keep me out of it. The horrid, nasty things!'

Now the toys didn't want the teddy bear to

see them building the brick house, or changing into their best clothes on Saturday afternoon in case he guessed their secret. So they decided to ask him to go out for a little walk, and then, while he was gone, they could get everything ready for his party.

So the sailor doll went to him on Saturday at two o'clock, and said kindly: 'Teddy, go for a little walk until four o'clock. It is a sunny afternoon and it will do you good.'

The teddy bear went red with rage. So they were going to get him out of the way, were they, while they were having their party! They were going to eat everything up! They weren't even going to let him *see* the party!

He rushed out of the door, with angry tears in his boot-button eyes. It was too bad! He'd run away! Yes, he would!

Off he went down the garden path. He walked and walked and walked. All the time he thought angrily about the toys.

'I *will* run away!' he said to himself. 'Yes, I will! But first I'll go back and tell the toys just what I think of them. I'll tell them how horrid they are – how unkind – how selfish! I'll go straight back now and tell them! Then I'll smack that sailor doll on the head and walk out with my nose in the air!'

Back he went to the nursery, quite determined to say some very horrid things. It was just four o'clock when he arrived; the toys had finished getting ready for the party, and were standing in a line ready to sing the song that the sailor doll had made up for them.

The bear stamped into the nursery and glared round at the toys.

'I've just come back to tell you what a lot of nast – ' he began – but he couldn't finish because at a sign from the sailor doll the toys opened their mouths and their beaks and began to sing very loudly:

> 'Here's a welcome hearty
> To your birthday party.
> Welcome, birthday-bear,
> Hurry up and share
> In our games and fun
> Till your birthday's done!'

Then they stopped, took a long breath and shouted: 'Many happy returns of the day, bear! Many happy returns of the day!'

They crowded round him shaking him by the paw, and the little pink rabbit gave him a hug!

The teddy bear was so surprised that at first he couldn't think what to say.

'But – but – but – is it my birthday?' he asked.

'Yes!' shouted the toys. 'And we hadn't forgotten it! We've been having secrets about it all the week. We were so afraid you'd guess. *Did* you guess?'

'Oh, no,' said the bear, going quite red to think of all the horrid things he had thought. 'I didn't guess for a minute.'

'Here's a nice blue birthday sash!' said the French doll. She wound it round his fat little body and tied it in a big bow. He looked beautiful.

'And here's a brooch – and a pair of blue shoes – and a fine walking-stick!' cried everyone, giving the surprised bear the presents. The shoes fitted him beautifully, and the brooch looked lovely just under his chin. As for the walking-stick he was as proud of it as he could be. Dear me, could all this be a dream? How lovely! What a silly bear he had been!

They had tea in the splendid brick house. The biscuits, cakes and sweets were most delicious, and the honey lemonade was so nice that the bear had five glasses of it and felt rather like a balloon at the end. But he was so happy that he didn't mind anything.

Then they had games, and after that the bear rode in the clockwork train six times round the nursery. That was lovely. Then he was presented with the chair that the pixie had made for him, and he was so surprised that he could hardly sit down in it! But he did, at last, and it was exactly the right size for him. His very own chair! How proud and pleased he was. He wanted to thank the pixie, so the little creature was called and came in to eat a chocolate bun.

He looked at the bear with a twinkle in his eye.

'Do you know,' he said solemnly, 'I saw a horrid little bear this afternoon, going along muttering the nastiest things about dolls, and sailor dolls, and ducks, and every sort of toy.'

The teddy bear looked as red as a tomato. How dreadful! The pixie must have seen him going for that walk!

'But it couldn't have been you, could it?' said the pixie, his bright eyes twinkling more than ever, as he looked at the bear. 'It must have been a foolish, sulky, stupid little bear who didn't know what he was talking about.'

'Yes, it was,' said the teddy bear humbly.

'Well, pixie, that little bear will never be so foolish again. I know the toys are my friends, and I will be a friend to them. They have given me a lovely birthday, and I will never forget it. It was a wonderful surprise.'

'Ah!' said the pixie wisely, smiling round at the listening toys. 'A surprise is a fine thing – isn't it, toys? It's a splendid cure for the mopes – and don't you forget it!'

The teddy bear never forgot it. He is always planning lovely surprises for everyone, and he never *thinks* of sulking in a corner now!

The Enchanted Doll

Mollie had a pretty doll called Angela, whom she loved very much indeed. She played with Angela all day long, and the only thing she wished was that Angela could talk and walk, instead of just lying or sitting perfectly still, and staring at Mollie with wide-open blue eyes.

'I can pretend you talk to me, and I can pretend you run about and play,' said Mollie, 'but you don't really and truly – and it *would* be such fun, Angela dear, if just for once in a way you would really come alive!'

But Angela just sat and stared, and didn't move a finger or say a word! It was most disappointing, for she really was a nice doll, and Mollie felt quite certain that if only she *could* talk and walk, she would be a good companion to have. Mollie had no brothers or sisters, so she was often lonely. That was why she played so much with Angela.

One day a very strange thing happened to Mollie. She took her doll for a walk in Pixie

Wood, and it happened there. Mollie had never seen any pixies or anything at all exciting in Pixie Wood, although it had such a lovely name. It was just like an ordinary wood.

But today it seemed a little different. The trees seemed closer together, as if they were nodding to one another, and whispering about something. The sun couldn't get in between the branches, and the wood was dim and rather mysterious. Mollie took Angela by the hand and walked her over the grass, talking to her. Her doll's pram was broken and had gone to be mended, which was why Angela was not riding in it as usual.

Mollie walked on through the wood – and then she suddenly stopped short. She saw something most surprising in the wood! It was a tiny pram, a little smaller than a doll's pram, and it shone like pure gold. It had a little white hood with a silver fringe hanging down, and the pram cover was white too, with gold embroidery on it. It really was very beautiful.

'Whatever is a doll's pram doing here in the middle of the wood?' wondered Mollie. 'I haven't seen any other children about. I wonder if they've left their pram here and are playing hide-and-seek or something. I'll cuckoo to them and see where they are. Perhaps they would let me play with them.'

So she called loudly: 'Cuckoo! Cuckoo! Where are you? Can I play with you?'

But there was no answer. The trees seemed to lean closer to one another, and all the leaves whispered again. Mollie looked all round and ran here and there, but it was no use at all – she couldn't see any children.

She looked at the lovely little pram. It was the nicest she had ever seen. How pretty Angela would look if she were tucked up in it and taken for a ride! Mollie went over to the pram and turned back the cover. There was no doll inside – but would you believe it, there was a little bottle there full of milk!

'But this pram can't belong to a *real* baby! It can't!' cried Mollie, in astonishment. 'It's too small. Oh! I wonder – I just wonder if it belongs to a pixie! It would be just right for a pixie baby. Oh, how lovely! I wish, I wish, I wish I could see a real pixie baby riding in that dear little pram!'

Mollie waited for a little while to see if any one came, but nobody did. Then a thought slid into her mind – would it matter if she put Angela into the pram and just wheeled her about for five minutes? Angela must be tired with her long walk, and really, she would look perfectly sweet in that pram! It wouldn't spoil the pram.

So Mollie picked up Angela and put her into the pram. She sat her down firmly, strapped her in, and set the soft pillow up behind her so that she could sit up comfortably. Then she tucked the white cover round her and began to wheel her about. How pretty Angela looked in the pixie pram! It was most exciting to wheel her about in it.

Mollie gave Angela a ride for a few minutes and then she thought she saw a little pointed face peeping at her from behind a tree.

'Who's there?' she called. 'Come and see Angela in this dear little pram, pixie!'

There was no answer – so Mollie left the pram and ran to the tree to see if the pixie really was peeping there. But, wasn't it disappointing, there was no one there at all, except a scurrying rabbit with a white bobtail!

Mollie turned back to the pram, and oh dear me, what a shock she got! The pram was running away! Yes, it really was! It was wheeling off all by itself, between the trees, as fast as ever it could!

'Oh! Oh! Come back, come back!' shouted

Mollie. 'Angela, Angela! Oh, please, pram, do come back! Don't take Angela away!'

But the pram hurried on. Mollie wondered if an invisible fairy was wheeling it, or whether the pram was a magic one that could go by itself. Oh, why, why had she put Angela in it! She ran after the hurrying pram as fast as ever she could, shouting as she went. The pram went faster and faster. It was dreadful. Mollie caught sight of the doll's face. It was full of horror and fear, and the little girl was sorry for her doll. She must, she really *must*, catch that pram!

The pram turned a corner by some thick bushes, and disappeared from sight. Mollie panted after it, but alas, when she reached the bushes, she could no longer see the pram. It was quite gone!

Mollie ran wildly about, and began to cry when she could not see the pram anywhere.

'Where have you gone, Angela?' she shouted. 'Can't you call and tell me?'

But there was no answer. Angela had disappeared with the pram. Mollie sat down and cried bitterly. It was dreadful to lose her doll like that. She did love her so much.

Presently she felt a little hand on her shoulder and a high, twittering voice said: 'What's the matter? Would you mind getting up? You are sitting on my front door.'

Mollie looked up in surprise. She saw a tiny creature by her, with long, pointed wings, pointed ears, and pointed shoes. It was smaller even than Angela, her doll, and was looking at her with big green eyes.

'Are you a pixie?' asked Mollie, in astonishment. 'How small you are! Am I really on your front door? I'm so sorry.'

She got up, and saw that she was sitting on a small yellow trap-door, sunk deeply into the ground. The pixie opened it and then looked at Mollie.

'Why are you crying?' he said.

Mollie told him all about the little pram she had found, and how it had run off with her doll.

'Oh, that pram belongs to Mother Dimity, the old woman who lives in a shoe,' said the pixie at once. 'She is very forgetful, you know, and leaves it about everywhere! If she goes home without it, she whistles for it and it goes to her of its own accord.'

'Well, it's taken my doll too,' said Mollie, beginning to cry again. Her tears fell in at the pixie's trap-door and he frowned.

'Please don't do that,' he said. 'You are

making my home all damp. Why are you crying now? You can easily go and find your doll. Mother Dimity will give her back if you ask her.'

'Where does she live?' asked Mollie.

'In the Shoe,' said the pixie, getting into his trap-door home. 'Knock at the Big Oak-Tree six times, go down the steps, find a boat to take you on the Underground River, and then ask the Wizard Who Grows Toadstools where the Shoe is. He is sure to know, because the Old Woman is his sister.'

'Thank you,' said Mollie, getting up. The pixie said goodbye and shut his trap-door with a bang. Mollie looked round for the Big Oak-Tree. There were a great many oak-trees around, and they all seemed about the same size to the little girl. She chose one that looked a little bigger than the others and knocked six times. Nothing happened at all. She knocked again. Still nothing happened.

'It can't be the right tree,' said Mollie, disappointed. She looked round again – and then she saw the biggest oak she had ever seen in her life! It was a real monster, towering up into the sky, and as big round as a summer-house!

'That's the one!' thought Mollie, and she ran over to it. She knocked on the trunk sharply six times – rat-tat-tat-tat-tat-tat! Then there came a creaking noise, and to her great delight a small door swung open in the tree and she saw that a narrow flight of steps led downwards towards the roots.

Her heart beat fast. This was a wonderful adventure! She slipped through the door, which at once shut with a bang, and began to go down the steps. It was rather dark, but small lanterns which hung here and there gave a little light. Mollie went down for a long way. She thought she must have climbed down quite a hundred steps when she came to a wide passage, with doors on every side. She looked at them. They all had names on, or messages written on little cards.

One card said: 'Ring, don't knock.' Another said: 'Knock, don't ring.' The next door had a card that said: 'Don't knock or ring,' and the fourth one said: 'I am not at home yesterday or tomorrow.'

Mollie thought that was strange, and she giggled. The names were strange too. 'Mister Woozle' was on one card, and 'Dame High-go-quick' was on another. Mollie read a third one, 'Little Jiggy-jig', and she was just wondering whatever he could be like when his door flew open and someone rushed out and nearly knocked her down. It was Little Jiggy-jig himself!

He was a funny fellow, with small wings, rabbit's ears and a funny habit of jigging up and down. 'Sorry!' he said to Mollie. 'Didn't see you there!'

He was just about to rush away when Mollie caught hold of his arm. 'Wait a minute,' she said. 'Could you please tell me if I am on the right way to the Underground River.'

'Yes, yes,' said Little Jiggy-jig, jerking his arm away impatiently. 'First to the right and left and then straight on round the corner.'

'But how can I go to the right and left at once, and how can anyone go straight round a corner!' called Mollie, indignantly. The only answer she got was a chuckle, and Little Jiggy-jig disappeared into the darkness of the passage. Mollie felt cross. She went straight on, and at last heard a noise of lapping water. 'That must be the Underground River,' she thought, pleased. 'Now to find a boat!'

She soon came to the river. It was hung with fairy lights of all colours and looked very pretty. There were plenty of boats on the side of it, but none of them had oars in them. Mollie looked about for someone to row her down the river, but she could see no one.

'Isn't there anyone here?' she shouted. Then a little head came poking out of a funny little ticket-office Mollie had not noticed.

'Yes, I'm here, and you're here too,' said the person in the ticket-office. Mollie went up and saw that it was a grey rabbit with a collar round its neck, and a tie flowing down, very neatly knotted.

'Good morning,' said Mollie. 'I want a boat.'

'Here's your ticket, then,' said the rabbit, handing her a very chewed-looking piece of cardboard.

'Where's the boatman?' asked Mollie.

'Nowhere,' said the rabbit. 'There isn't one.'

'Then how can I go in a boat?' asked Mollie.

'Get in it yourself, silly,' said the rabbit.

'Don't be rude,' said Mollie. 'It's no use taking a boat if you haven't got oars, is it? Silly yourself!'

'Now who's being rude!' said the rabbit. 'You are being very simple, little girl. Why do you want to take a boat? Why not let the boat take *you*?'

Mollie glared at the rabbit, and then walked

up to one of the boats. She chose a blue one, dotted with gold stars and got into it. At once the boat glided off by itself.

'Good morning, good afternoon and good evening!' shouted the rabbit, but Mollie didn't answer. She thought he was rather silly.

The boat shot on down the river, and after a little while it left the underground darkness and came out into the open air. Mollie blinked in the bright sunshine, but she was very glad indeed to be in the light again. The boat sped on and on, and Mollie watched the strange folk walking in the flowery fields, and saw with surprise that the animals were dressed up like human beings.

The boat went on, rocking gently. Mollie suddenly saw a curious field, with a strange-looking old man waving a stick about in the middle of it. He was surrounded by toadstools of all sizes, colours, and shapes, and she knew that he must be the Wizard Who Grows Toadstools.

'Stop, stop!' she cried to the boat. It stopped at once and headed to the bank. Mollie patted it, said thank you and then jumped out. She went to the old wizard, who didn't see her at first and almost knocked her over with his waving stick, which the little girl now saw was a silver wand.

'Please,' she said. 'I've come to ask you where your sister, the old woman who lives in a shoe, is. I want to go and speak to her.'

'You'll find her on the other side of that hill,' said the wizard, waving his wand violently, and nearly catching Mollie in the eye with it. 'Look out! You are standing just where my next toadstool is growing!'

Mollie felt the earth pushing up under her feet and fell over. A big toadstool appeared through the ground and grew high and broad. It was covered with big red spots. Mollie sat on the ground and watched it in amazement. Then she felt the earth moving just under her again, and at once she was shot up high on another growing toadstool.

'Well, really,' said the wizard, in disgust, 'how you do get in the way, to be sure! Mind where you tread as you go through the field. There are toadstools growing everywhere today, for I have a very large order for them from the King himself, who wants three hundred for stools for his next party.'

Mollie ran out of the field as quickly as she could, and made her way to the hill in the distance. She climbed it, and as soon as she came to the top she saw the Shoe. It was an

enormous shoe, and it had windows and doors in it and a smoking chimney at the top. Mollie thought it looked lovely. She ran down to it, and at once she was surrounded by a crowd of small pixie children, not so big as she was, with pointed faces, pointed ears, and short wings.

'Who are you? Where do you come from?' they cried in excitement. 'Have you come to see our new child?'

'Look, our new little girl is in bed! You can see her through the window!' said a tiny pixie, taking Mollie's hand and leading her to a window that looked into the Shoe house. Mollie peeped in – and whatever *do* you think she saw? She saw a bedroom in the Shoe, with many little white beds in it, and in one of them, the bed nearest to the window, lay Angela, her own little doll!

'Do you see that new little girl?' said the pixie. 'Well, she came in today in Mother Dimity's pram, and do you know, she is very ill, poor thing! She can't talk, she can't eat, she can't drink, she can't even blink her eyes! Isn't it dreadful! I've never seen a little girl like that before, have you?'

'That isn't a little girl at all, that's my doll!' cried Mollie.

'A doll!' said the pixie children, crowding round Mollie. 'What's a doll? We don't know what a doll is.'

'Well, a doll is – a doll is – well, that's what a doll is!' said Mollie, pointing to where Angela lay on the little bed.

'But can't the poor thing move or talk at all?' asked the pixies in surprise.

'Of course not,' said Mollie. 'I'm going in to get Angela. Poor darling, she must feel so frightened!'

She ran in at the door of the big Shoe, and bumped into the Old Woman.

'Now then, gently, gently!' said Mother Dimity. 'You'll frighten the new little girl, rushing about like that. I've just given her some very strong magic medicine to make her come alive again.'

'She never has been alive!' cried Mollie. 'She's my doll!'

'Your doll!' said the Old Woman. 'Doll! Oh, I remember once seeing a doll in the world of boys and girls. Dear, dear me, so that's a doll, is it? Why, I thought it was a little girl that was ill, and so I've given her some stuff to make her walk and talk. I'm really very sorry indeed.'

'But, do you mean to say that Angela will soon walk and talk?' cried Mollie.

'Of course,' said Mother Dimity. 'Look – she is blinking her eyes now! Perhaps I had better make her go back into a doll again.'

'No, please don't,' said Mollie at once. She ran to Angela and looked at her. Wonder of wonders, the little doll was opening and shutting her eyes and she suddenly looked at Mollie and smiled a wide smile, showing all her pretty teeth.

'Hello, Mollie,' she said. 'I've often wanted to talk to you, and now I can!'

Mollie watched her in amazement. Angela threw back the covers and jumped out of bed. She danced round the room in joy and then ran up to Mollie. She hugged the little girl's legs, and Mollie lifted her up into her arms. She was so pleased to have Angela back, walking and talking, that the tears ran down her cheeks in joy.

'Oh, what fun we'll have together now!' she cried, hugging her doll to her. 'We can talk to one another, and play all kinds of games.'

'But you mustn't let anyone but yourself know,' said Mother Dimity at once. 'If you do, the magic will go, and Angela will be an ordinary doll again.'

'Oh, I won't tell anyone at all!' said Mollie, happily. 'Come on, Angela, we'll go home again now. It must be getting late.'

She put the little doll on the ground and Angela took her hand. Then, walking like a real person, she trotted beside Mollie, saying goodbye to all the pixie children.

Mother Dimity showed them a short way home, and they arrived there just in time for dinner. Mollie put Angela in her cot, and told her to be sure not to move if anyone came in, and she promised.

And now Mollie is as happy as the day is long, for she has a real, live doll to play with her, and they *do* have some fine games together.

'Really,' Mollie's mother often says, 'you might think that doll was alive, the way Mollie plays with her all day long!'

And then Mollie smiles a big smile – but she doesn't say a word! She has a wonderful secret to keep and she keeps it very well!

When the Toys Came Alive

Once upon a time there were two children called Peter and Gwen. They lived in a big house, and had a wonderful nursery full of marvellous toys. There was a rocking-horse far bigger than themselves, with a long tail and mane, and fine brown eyes that opened and shut as he rocked to and fro. There was a doll's house with electric light in every room, a bathroom with taps that really ran water, and fires that could really be lit. There were all sorts and kinds of dolls, animals and books.

They really were very lucky children, but you know, they had too many toys! They had so many that they didn't really love any of them, except two very old and ragged creatures that they had taken to bed with them ever since they were two years old.

These old creatures were so battered and worn that it was hard to tell that one had once been a monkey and the other had been a cat. When the children had had these toys their parents had not been rich, and the children had had few toys then – so they loved the two creatures, and always cuddled them at night.

But when they grew rich and went to live in a great big house, and had a nanny to look after them, they became spoilt and horrid. They had new toys every day and they didn't take care of any of them. I couldn't tell you how many they broke or how many they threw out of the window just for fun. It really was dreadful.

Once Peter wound up his clockwork engine with all its trucks behind it and set it going towards the pond in the garden. Splish-splash! The engine and all its trucks disappeared into the water at once, and when it was fished out a week later it was rusty and useless, and could never be wound up again.

Another time Gwen threw every one of her dolls out of the nursery window to the ground far below, and, of course, they were all broken to bits. Really, you would hardly believe the horrid, unkind things that those two children did to their toys.

But something happened one day – something very strange and peculiar. The children were playing in the nursery when they found a bag of little yellow sweets in the toy cupboard.

They were most surprised.

'How did they get there?' asked Peter.

'I don't mind where they came from but I know where they're going to!' said Gwen, and she popped four or five of the little sweets into her mouth. They tasted delicious and she took some more. Peter took some too.

And then they noticed a very alarming thing. The nursery seemed to be getting much bigger! The table looked enormous, and the chairs seemed far too big to sit on. The waste-paper basket looked big enough to hide in without being seen, and the flowers in the vase seemed like giant ones.

'What's happened?' said Peter, looking round in dismay. 'Why is everything so big?'

'I do believe it's us that have gone small!' said Gwen, staring round in astonishment. 'It must be those sweets, Peter. We shouldn't have eaten them. They were magic ones, I'm sure!'

Just at that moment their nanny came into the room and the children, now as small as tiny dolls, ran over to her, calling out. But their voices were squeaky now, and the nanny, who was short-sighted, thought they were mice. So she took up the hearth-brush and shooed them away, crying: 'You nasty horrid little mice! I'll set a trap for you, that I will!'

Peter was swept up by the brush and fell to the floor. He scrambled into a house of bricks that he and Gwen had built that morning. The little girl followed him and they hid there, trembling, until their nanny had gone out of the room.

'Whatever are we to do?' asked Gwen, at last. But, before she could answer, a furry face peeped in at the door of the little brick house, and gave her a dreadful fright.

'It's all right, it's only the teddy bear,' said Peter, taking a good look at him. 'He looks big because we're so small now.'

'*Only* the teddy bear!' said the furry face, crossly. 'I'll teach you to say I'm *only* the teddy bear!' and with that he pushed over the house of bricks so that it came toppling round the children's ears. Crack! Smack! The hard wooden bricks hit the children and made them squeal. The teddy bear danced for joy and called to the other toys to come and see.

'You horrid, unkind thing!' shouted Peter, crawling out from beneath the pile of bricks.

'Well, it's just what you did to me and the brown toy dog yesterday!' said the teddy bear, grinning. 'Tit for tat, you know! Wait till the rocking-horse catches sight of you. He's king of this nursery, and he has been in a very bad temper ever since you and your sister pulled all the hairs out of his tail.'

At the mention of his name the rocking-horse turned his head and looked straight down at the two children. He looked so big and fierce that they trembled in their shoes.

'Hrrrrumph!' he said, in a horsy voice. 'What's all this?'

'Do look, your majesty,' said the teddy bear, excited. 'Here are the two children gone small. They've eaten those magic sweets that the pixies left in the toy cupboard last night. They are smaller than we are!'

'Hrrrrrrumph!' said the rocking-horse again. 'Call a meeting. This is important. We may be able to punish these children for all the unkind things they have done to their helpless toys. Hrrrrrrumph!'

The teddy bear bowed to the big horse, and hurried off to the toy cupboard. Out came toy animals of all kinds, an old engine, a motorbus, four dolls, all with broken arms or legs or noses, twenty-four soldiers, marching in two straight lines, and all the wooden animals out of the Noah's ark.

They really were a sight to see. They all went to the rocking-horse and bowed to him.

'Hrrrrrumph!' he snorted at them. 'For a long time, Gwen and Peter, we toys have been in your power. Now, for a change, you are in ours. You have always been unkind to us. We shall now be unkind to you, then you will know what it feels like. Hrrrrrmph!'

'Oh please, don't hurt us!' begged Gwen, beginning to cry. 'We never really hurt *you*, you know.'

'Do you suppose I liked having all the hairs pulled out of my beautiful tail?' shouted the rocking-horse angrily. 'Teddy, pull a few hairs out of the girl's head. She can then see if it hurts.'

The teddy bear pulled a few hairs sharply out of Gwen's head and she squealed in pain. 'Don't! It hurts.'

'You pulled *all* the hairs out of my tail,' said the rocking-horse. 'I can't make up my mind whether to have all the hairs pulled out of your head or not.'

'Oh no, no!' cried Gwen, really very frightened. 'Do forgive me, please. I should look dreadful without any hair.'

'So do *I* look dreadful without any hairs in my

tail,' said the rocking-horse, gloomily. 'Well, toys, you had better take these children to Toytown, and we'll ask the toy judge there to say what had better be done to such unkind children.'

'Could we go on your back?' asked the teddy bear. 'We could get there so much more quickly if we could ride.'

'Jump up, then,' said the rocking-horse. Then with shouts of delight all the toys climbed up on to the wide back of the big rocking-horse. Gwen and Peter were pulled up too.

'HRRRRRRRRUMPH!' snorted the rocking-horse loudly, and he suddenly rocked himself right out of the nursery door, down the stairs, and out into the garden at top speed. Gwen couldn't help wondering what Nanny would say if she met them – but they didn't meet anybody.

The horse rocked down the garden and out of the gate at the bottom. It rocked down the lane and came to the wood. It rocked down a narrow path and went deeper and deeper into the wood. At last it came to a high gate. It knocked on this, with its head, and the gate swung open.

Gwen and Peter saw that they had come to Toytown. It was a queer place. The houses and shops were made of wood and cardboard and were exactly like toy ones. The trees were like the funny stiff ones in their toy farm at home, and the people walking about the streets were all toys. They stared hard when they saw the rocking-horse coming down the street.

At last the horse came to a tall building, and on the front was its name, Toytown Hall. All the toys got off the rocking-horse, pulled Gwen and Peter with them, and went into the hall. Gwen and Peter looked round. The hall was a big place with a platform at one end, and plenty of forms for people to sit on.

'The judge will be here in a minute,' whispered the teddy bear to the others. Sure enough in a short while there came the sound of heavy footsteps, and into the hall marched a toy judge, in a long, flowing gown and a thick white wig. He looked very fierce and grand. The toys all got up and bowed to him. Gwen and Peter thought they had better do so, too.

The judge sat on a throne-like chair on the platform and looked all round, frowning.

'Any complaints today?' he asked in a rumbling voice. At once all the toys jumped up and shouted, 'YES!'

'Quiet,' said the judge. 'One at a time, please. Rocking-horse, what is all this about?'

'Please, your worship,' said the rocking-horse, 'we have brought two bad children here to be judged by you. They have eaten magic sweets, become small, and so are in our power. How shall we punish them?'

'Well, what have they done to *you*?' asked the judge, biting the end of his pen.

'If you please, your worship, the boy wound up his engine, and sent it, with its trucks, right into a big pond of water,' said the teddy bear, jumping up like a jack-in-the-box.

'Truly shocking,' said the judge.

'And if you please, your worship, the girl threw all her dolls out of a high window to see if they would break,' said the rabbit, bobbing up excitedly.

'Then for punishment tie the boy in a railway train, wind it up and send it into a pond with him,' said the judge, writing busily. 'See how he likes it. And for the girl, take her up to the top of a high building and throw her out of the window to see if she breaks.'

'Ooooooh!' squealed the two children, in despair. 'Your worship, forgive us! We are not toys, we shall drown, we shall break out arms and legs.'

'Take them away,' said the judge sternly.

'No, no, have mercy on us!' shouted Peter. 'We will never be unkind again. We didn't know toys minded. Just give us a chance and we will be kind.'

'Have you *ever* been kind?' asked the judge, sternly.

'Of course,' said Peter.

'Then listen,' said the judge, 'if any toy will come forward to say you have been kind to him, then you shall go free. Now then, who will speak for these children?'

Peter and Gwen looked round at their toys – but not one of them moved! No, they just sat there on the forms, staring in front of them, not one with a kind word to say about the two children.

'Very well,' said the judge frowning. 'The two children must be punished as I said. Take them away.'

Gwen began to cry, and Peter bit his lip hard. What a dreadful fix to be in! It was no use trying to run away, and not a bit of good fighting the toys, for now they were bigger even than the children! Peter and Gwen were as much in the toys' power as once the toys had been in theirs. Things were certainly topsy turvy!

The toys dragged the children out of the town

hall and then stood outside talking about what to do next.

'There's an old train that lives near the big duck-pond not far off,' said the teddy bear. 'We'll take Peter to that.'

'Yes, and there's a tall tower not far from the old train!' said the rocking-horse, in his deep voice. 'We will take Gwen to the top of that.'

'Boo-hoo-hoo!' wept Gwen in fright. 'I don't want to be thrown out of the window.'

'Nor did your dolls,' said the brown dog, sternly. 'But it didn't make any difference. You threw them out!'

The toys took the children down a lane and out into a field. Nearby was a large pond on which toy ducks were bobbing up and down happily. An old engine with two trucks stood on a pair of rails a little way from the pond. Just behind rose a tall thin tower with a window at the top.

Gwen was hustled into the tower and made to climb a steep winding stair. When she looked out of the window at the top she saw that Peter was tightly tied to the engine, and the engine was being wound up so that it could go puffing into the pond.

'Ooooh, oooh!' wept Gwen.

'Now, are you all ready?' shouted the rocking-horse. The teddy bear caught hold of Gwen's arm, ready to push her out of the window, and the brown dog below finished winding up the big clockwork engine.

And, just at that very moment two strange creatures came into sight down the lane. They were hurrying as fast as they could, and as they ran they shouted something at the top of their voices.

The toys stared and listened. What was all this? They had no idea who the strange, shapeless creatures were.

But Peter knew! Gwen knew!

'Oh, it's dear old Monkey, that I used to take to bed with me!' cried Peter.

'And it's darling old Pussy that I used to cuddle each night!' shouted Gwen. 'Pussy, Pussy, come and save us!'

'Monkey, tell these toys to untie me!' shouted Peter, struggling hard to get free. But the toys held him tightly.

'Hi, toys, hi, toys, wait a bit, wait a bit!' yelled the two hurrying creatures. 'We've got something to say!'

The toys waited. When the two creatures came up the toys saw that they had once been toy animals, but were now very battered and worn.

'What do you want?' asked the rocking-horse with a snort.

'We've only just heard that Gwen and Peter are going to be punished unless a toy will speak for them and say that they have been kind,' panted the monkey. 'Well, we've come to speak for them.'

'To speak for Gwen and Peter!' cried all the toys, in astonishment. 'How surprising! Do you mean to say that these two unkind children were ever kind to you?'

'Kind! I should think so!' said the cat, mopping her hot forehead. 'Why, they loved us better than anything and took us to bed each night for years. It wasn't till last year that their nanny said we were too old and dirty to be in their clean beds any more, and she wanted to throw us into the dustbin. But Gwen and Peter wouldn't let her. They hid us away in the boot-cupboard, and do you know, they sometimes take us out, even now, and cuddle us at night when their nanny is away for her weekend!'

'It's true, quite true,' said the monkey, swinging what was left of his tail. 'I dare say the children have been unkind to *you*, toys – when people get rich they often change for the worse, you know – but both the cat and I must truthfully say that we have been loved and cared for by Gwen and Peter for a good many years. We don't want you to punish them. Please don't. We love them, you see, and we know that if children have been kind once they can be again. Give them a chance. I'm sure they will never, never be unkind to anything or anyone again.'

The toys talked together.

'Well, you know what the judge said,' said the rocking-horse, snorting loudly. 'If any toy would say a kind word for the children they should go free. So we can't punish them now. We must set them free.'

They untied Peter and took Gwen down the winding stair to the bottom of the tower. Both the children rushed gladly at their two old toys and hugged them until the monkey and the cat squealed for breath.

'Oh, you saved us just in time. I don't care what Nanny says, I'm going to have you in bed every single night, you dear old cuddlesome things!' cried Gwen.

'They look very battered and old,' said the rocking-horse, suddenly. 'How is it you didn't take better care of them? Look at the cat. She's a perfect sight, and hasn't even a whisker. And as for the monkey, he may call that a tail that he's got at the back, but *I* don't. It seems to me that you weren't very kind to these two toys, for all they say, children!'

'We're battered and old because we've been played with and loved such a lot,' said the monkey, at once, and he jerked his little bit of a tail up and down nimbly. 'Don't you know the difference between a broken toy and a well-used one? Look at this patch here on my back. I had a hole there and Gwen mended me. And look at the cat's ear. It came off, and Peter stuck it on again most beautifully. Oh, I can tell you, we're happy toys and have nothing to complain of except that we don't see our children often enough!'

'You shall see us every day and every night now!' cried Peter and Gwen. Then they linked arms with the two old toys and walked proudly off with them, all the toys following. The rocking-horse called to everyone to get on to his back again and up they all climbed, Peter and Gwen too. Then back they went to the nursery, rocking away hard.

When they were safely back again the

rocking-horse told Gwen and Peter to sit down on the floor with their eyes shut while he sang a magic song. They did so – and dear me, what an astonishing thing, when they opened their eyes again, they were the right size – just as big as ever! Their toys seemed very small to them.

'Oh, Peter!' cried Gwen. 'What a strange adventure! Let's be kind to everything now, shall we? It's much nicer than being horrid. Whatever should we have done without Monkey and Pussy?'

'Hrrrrrrrrrumph! said the rocking-horse loudly – but that was the last time he ever spoke!

The Brownie Who Pulled Faces

There was once a brownie called Twisty, who could pull the most dreadful faces you can imagine. It really was terrible to see him!

He could roll his eyes. He could screw up his nose till it looked like a withered apple. He could blow out his cheeks and he could pull down his mouth and make himself look most frightening.

Twisty thought it was funny to pull faces. He liked to meet a crowd of little pixies and stand in front of them, pulling the most dreadful faces he could think of. It frightened them very much indeed.

Nothing could stop him! Bron, the head brownie of the village of Puff, where Twisty lived, was always telling him to stop. His old aunt Chiffle-Chuffle shook her head at him and said he would make his face very ugly. And his next-door neighbour, Woof, said he would call in the policeman if he caught Twisty pulling faces at his baby in the garden.

Now one day old Witch Henny-penny came to stay for two days in Puff Village. She went out walking one morning and she met Twisty. She was a polite old dame, so she wished him good day.

Twisty thought it would be funny to give her a scare. So he turned up his nose, rolled his eyes round and put out his long, pointed tongue. The old witch watched him in silence.

Then she spoke in her deep, hoarse voice.

'Not very nice, not very pretty, and certainly most rude,' she said. 'One day the wind will change when you are pulling faces, brownie, and then you will be sorry.'

'Why shall I be sorry?' asked Twisty, surprised.

'Because whoever is making a face when the wind changes cannot pull his face right again,' said the witch solemnly. 'If your tongue should be out when the wind shifts from east to south, it will stay out! If your cheeks are blown out like a balloon, they will stay like that! You be careful, brownie! One day you'll be pulling a face when the wind changes and what a shock you will get!'

Twisty didn't believe her. He made an ugly face again.

'You're just making it up to frighten me!' he said. 'But I'm not frightened of the wind! Ho ho! You're a silly old witch, and I'm not afraid of you either!'

The witch looked strangely at Twisty. Her eyes seemed to go right through him – deeper, deeper, deeper, and the foolish brownie felt odd. He ran home quickly, looking behind him now and again to make sure the witch was not looking after him still!

He soon forgot what she had said. Two days later he was talking to a visitor at his front door. He thought it would be very funny to make a face at him, to give him a surprise. So he blew out his cheeks and sent his eyebrows right up to his hair. He waggled his pointed ears and made them stick straight out from his head instead of upwards. His visitor gaped in surprise and then looked offended.

'How dare you make a face at me!' he cried. 'I shall complain about you. Yes, I will!'

Twisty was just going to pull his face right again when something happened – the wind changed! The weathercock on the town hall swung round from east to west, just as Twisty made that face

Twisty couldn't think why he couldn't stop

his cheeks from blowing themselves out. He couldn't make his ears stop waggling, nor could he make them point upwards. His eyebrows wouldn't come down again – they stuck up high on his head and gave him a most peculiar look.

Twisty began to feel frightened. He glanced up at the weathercock and saw that the wind had changed all at once. He remembered what the old witch had said and a cold shiver ran down his back. Ooh! Supposing she had spoken the truth! How dreadful!

He slammed his front door, much to his visitor's surprise, and ran to the kitchen. He took down a looking-glass, and looked at himself. Yes, it was quite true – he could not stop pulling that dreadful face! It was stuck like that.

'Oh dear! Oh my! Goodness, gracious, whatever shall I do?' groaned Twisty, in dismay.

His ears waggled and waggled. His cheeks stayed blown out. He really did look dreadful.

The worst of it was that Twisty was going to a party that very afternoon at Bron's. Could he go now? Would it matter if he went with his face like that?

'Perhaps it will go right again before this

afternoon,' said Twisty, wishing his ears would stop waggling.

But his face didn't go right. It stayed just like it was. Twisty changed into his green velvet party-tunic and stared at himself once more in the glass. He was more used to his strange-looking, blown-out face by this time, and he thought perhaps people wouldn't notice it very much. He could say he had toothache. That would be a naughty story, but Twisty wasn't always careful to tell the truth.

So off he went to the party, his ears waggling so hard that he couldn't keep his hat on for more than half a minute at a time. He shook hands with Bron, who stared at him very hard. Then Twisty went to join the others, who wanted to play a game of oranges and lemons.

Everyone stared at Twisty and he felt very hot and uncomfortable. At last a small elf came up to him and said: 'Why are you making such a dreadful face? Don't you feel well?'

'Not very,' said Twisty.

'Why are your cheeks blown out like that?' asked a gnome.

'I've got toothache,' said Twisty, going red.

'Why do your ears waggle?' asked a brownie. 'Have you got earache too?'

'I expect I have,' said Twisty.

'And what has happened to your eyebrows?' said a pixie, peering up at him. 'You don't seem to have any. You are a very strange-looking and ugly brownie. Are you sure you haven't been pulling faces? The wind changed very suddenly this morning, and perhaps it just caught you pulling a face!'

Everyone came round Twisty and began to laugh. They were all quite certain that that was what had happened. Twisty stood there feeling miserable.

'Well, well,' said Bron, shaking his head at Twisty. 'It's time you were taught a lesson, Twisty. I'm not sorry you've been caught like this! You won't pull ugly faces again in a hurry!'

'How can I get rid of this one and make my face nice again?' asked poor Twisty.

'Well, as the Wind made your face stick like that, I should think that only the Wind can make it come right again,' said Bron. 'I'd go and see if the Wind could help you, if I were you. You know where he lives, don't you? On the top of Breezy Hill, just outside Fairyland. You can't possibly go about looking as ugly as you are now. I wouldn't let you live in our village!'

Twisty ran out of the house, crying. He went

home and packed his bag. Then he set out on the long journey to Breezy Hill. At last he left Fairyland behind and came to the long, steep hill. Up he climbed and up and up. At the top was a long flight of slippery steps, and beyond these was the cloud-like castle of the Wind. It was forever changing its shape, and was marvellous to see.

Twisty knocked at the great gate. It swung open and he went inside. He stood in a big hall, and although he looked all round it, it seemed to be empty.

A small mouse was nibbling some crumbs on the floor. Twisty spoke to it.

'Where is the Wind? Is he here today?'

'Not yet,' said the mouse. 'He'll be here at any moment. He hasn't been in a very good temper lately, so if I were you I wouldn't make that dreadful face at him. He might be very angry with you.'

Twisty felt rather frightened. But it was no use, he simply could *not* stop his ears from waggling, his eyebrows from raising themselves high up on his forehead, and his cheeks from blowing themselves out. The little mouse stared at him for a few moments and then ran to its hole in fright. It really thought Twisty must be mad.

The brownie looked round the hall, wishing the Wind would come – and almost at once he did! There was suddenly a great draught, and all the curtains blew straight up in the air. The door banged loudly and the carpets flew across the floor. Then Twisty saw the Wind.

He was an enormous fellow, dressed in cloud-like clothes that swayed out round him all the time. His hair was long and curly and his eyes flashed like lightning. He saw Twisty as soon as he entered the hall and stood still in surprise.

'Who are you?' he bellowed.

'Twisty the brownie,' said the frightened brownie. 'I've c-c-c-come to ask you if you'll be k-k-k-kind enough t-t-t-to – '

'Stop waggling your ears at me!' roared the Wind angrily. 'How rude of you! Stop it, I say!'

'I c-c-c-c-can't,' stammered Twisty.

'Nonsense!' cried the Wind, jumping up and standing over the trembling brownie. 'If you don't stop your ears waggling at me, *I'll* soon stop them for you.'

Poor Twisty tried his hardest to put his ears straight up and stop them from waggling, but he couldn't. The Wind lost his temper and gave Twisty a big box on each of his ears – clip, clap! The brownie cried out in pain – but dear me, his ears had stopped waggling! Yes, they really had.

'And now stop blowing your cheeks out at me,' roared the Wind again. 'Stop it, I say!'

'I c-c-c-c-can't!' began Twisty, wishing he could run away.

'*I'll* soon stop you!' cried the rough Wind, and he slapped Twisty once on each cheek – slip, slap!

'Ooh!' cried Twisty, dancing about in pain. 'Ooh!'

But certainly his cheeks stopped blowing themselves out at once! They put themselves right again and stayed right.

'And now, where are your eyebrows?' asked the Wind. 'You are making faces at me, are you? First you waggle your ears, then you blow out your cheeks, and then you raise your eyebrows at me and look down your nose! Ho ho!'

'Please, please,' said Twisty, going down on his knees to the Wind. 'Don't be rough with me any more. I came to ask you for help.'

The Wind laughed, and then opened his big mouth.

'I don't help people who pull faces!' he said. 'Look out for your eyebrows, brownie! I'm going to blow them off!'

He began to blow. My, how he blew! The brownie felt himself rising in the air. He felt his nose being bent crooked. He felt his hair being blown straight up. He felt his eyebrows being blown right off! Then out of the door he flew, a great draught down the back of his neck!

The Wind blew and blew until a great gale came sweeping up and around the palace. Twisty was caught by it and rolled down the long flight of slippery steps. Bump! Bump! Bump!

All the way down the steps he went and rolled to the bottom of Breezy Hill.

'Ho ho ho!' roared the Wind. 'That will teach you to come pulling faces at me, brownie!'

Poor Twisty. He was bruised all over. He had lost his eyebrows and his hair was blown straight up on end. He limped home with his bag and went into his cottage.

There came a knock at his door. It was Bron, the chief brownie.

'Have you come back all right?' he asked. 'Is your face right again?'

'My ears are all right and so are my cheeks,' said Twisty. 'But my eyebrows are gone and I am all over bruises. I shall never, never, never pull faces again, Bron.'

'Dear, dear,' said Bron, looking at him. 'You certainly do look strange with your hair on end and your eyebrows gone – but never mind, you can brush your hair flat and your eyebrows will grow again. Cheer up! I expect you will be much nicer now!'

Twisty *is* much nicer, and he has never been seen to pull an ugly face again. Mind you don't either, just in *case* the wind might suddenly change when you do it; because that really would be dreadful, wouldn't it?

All the Way to Toytown

One morning Roger thought he would go for a ride in his little motor-car. It was a fine car, painted a bright green, and it had a hooter, two lamps, and a little extra seat at the back for one passenger. Roger was very proud of it. He had had the motor for his birthday, and he could work the pedals so quickly that the car shot along the road at a tremendous pace!

'I'm just going for a ride, Mummy!' he called to his mother, climbing into his car. 'I shan't be long.'

Off he went, pedalling fast down the lane. He thought he would go through the wood. The path was narrow, but just big enough for his little motor-car. There might perhaps be a few blackberries just beginning to get ripe.

Into the dim green wood he went. A rabbit ran across the path and Roger hooted at it, 'honk, honk!' He didn't want to run over a bunny! On and on he went and at last stopped in surprise.

He must have taken the wrong turning! He

didn't seem to know this part of the wood at all! He began to turn his car round so that he could go back – and it was just then that he heard the sound of someone crying nearby.

'What's that, I wonder?' said Roger to himself. 'Perhaps it is somebody lost.'

He jumped out of his car and went to see. Behind a tree he saw a small and very pretty little girl, her golden hair all over her face, as she bent her head and cried into a little pink handkerchief.

'I say!' called Roger. 'What's the matter? Are you lost?'

'No,' said the little girl, looking up in surprise. 'I know my way all right, but I can't walk any farther. So I'm crying because I am unhappy.'

'Why can't you walk?' asked Roger. 'Have you hurt your foot?'

'Well, you see, my leg has come right off,' said the little girl, much to Roger's astonishment. 'Don't look so surprised, boy. I'm not a little girl – I'm a doll, and dolls' legs easily come off, you know, if people are careless with them.'

'A doll!' said Roger, still more astonished. 'I didn't know dolls could walk and talk.'

'Well, they can't usually,' said the doll. 'Only when something important has happened. You see, Mary, the little girl I belong to, dropped me yesterday and my leg almost broke in half. So last night I made up my mind to go to Toytown and get it mended. They have a fine dolls' hospital there. But on my way my leg got worse and now, look, it's come right off!'

Roger looked – yes, it was true. The doll's leg *had* come off. No wonder she couldn't walk any more!

'Won't it push back into place?' he said, knowing that sometimes the arms and legs of dolls could be mended like that. But the doll shook her head.

'I'm afraid not,' she said. 'I'm not that sort of doll. But really, I don't know what in the world to do! I can't walk back home to Mary, and I can't get to Toytown. And if I stay here I shall be ill with cold and loneliness!'

'Where is Toytown?' asked Roger. 'If you know the way perhaps I could take you there in my motor-car.'

'Ooh! What a lovely plan!' cried the doll, delighted. 'I didn't know you had a motor-car. I thought you were just walking. Of course you can take me, if you don't mind!'

Roger helped the doll to her one foot. She carried her broken leg under her arm and didn't

really seem to mind much about it. She hopped
to the car and got into the little seat at the back.
Roger climbed into his seat and pedalled off
through the wood.

The doll knew her way very well indeed.
'Now round this beech tree,' she said. 'Now
keep straight on till you come to a little gorse
bush. Now to the left by that hazel. Now round
the corner by that tiny stream. You'll have to go
through it, but it is very shallow. That's right!
Now straight on till we come to a lane.'

At last they came to a winding lane. On one
side there was a farm, and Roger thought it
really looked exactly like his toy farm at home,
even to the funny stiff trees that seemed to grow
from the round piece of wood at the bottom and
not from the ground itself. White celluloid
ducks swam on a pond, and they quacked as
loudly as real ducks, but sounded rather hollow.

As they drew nearer to Toytown itself Roger
was surprised to see a large crowd on the road.
He hooted a great many times and the people
got out of the way. They were strange-looking
folk – all of them toys of various sizes. Some
were small and some were as large as Roger
himself. There were ducks dressed up, rabbits
in coats and trousers, dolls of all kinds, a clown

or two, a large pink cat whose ears wagged to
and fro as he walked, and many other toys.

'Oh, dear! It's market-day in Toytown today,'
said the doll, suddenly. 'I wondered why there
were so many people. What a nuisance! I don't
expect the hospital will be open. It shuts on
Sundays and market-days.'

'But hospitals never shut!' said Roger, in
surprise.

'Toy hospitals do,' said the doll. 'Now I shall
have to wait till tomorrow to get my leg mended.
What a nuisance!'

They drove into Toytown. It was a marvellous
place! Roger could quite well see that every
house, every shop, every farm was built of bricks
or meccano. But they were all a good size, far
bigger than toys. There was a wooden policeman
in the market-square, and he stopped Roger as
he pedalled along in his motor-car.

'You're going too fast!' he said, sternly. 'It's
market-day today, so there's a low speed-limit.'

'Oh, policeman, is the hospital shut?' asked
the doll, leaning out.

'Of course,' said the policeman.

'Is there anywhere I can stay for the night?'
asked the doll. 'I want to get my leg mended
tomorrow.'

'You might try at the big farm over there,' said the policeman, pointing to a fine toy-farm not far off. 'I know Mrs Straws has a few beds for visitors.'

'Would you drive me there, Roger, and go and ask the farmer's wife if she can let me stay the night?' asked the doll. Roger at once drove over to the farmhouse and got out at the little wooden gate. Toy cows and toy horses made of wood were everywhere. They ran up to him like dogs and seemed delighted to see him. He pushed them away and went up to the front door of the farmhouse. He knocked loudly.

Mrs Straws came to the door. She was just like the farmer's wife in Roger's farm at home. In fact, she was *so* like her that he really wondered for a moment if she had run away and come to Toytown.

'What is it you want?' she asked.

'Could you let a doll with a broken leg stay here for the night?' asked Roger. Mrs Straws shook her head.

'I'm sorry,' she said, 'but all my beds are quite full up tonight. It's market-day, you know, and Toytown is always crowded then. I'm afraid you won't find a bed anywhere at all.'

Roger went back to the car and told the doll.

Her big blue eyes filled with tears. 'What am I to do?' she said. 'I must sleep somewhere for the night.'

The farmer's wife came up to the car when she saw the doll crying. 'Don't upset yourself,' she said. 'You can easily get a box of bricks from the store-keeper in the middle of the town, and surely this boy can build you a nice little house for the night!'

That *did* sound a splendid idea! Roger climbed into his car again and drove the doll to the store-keeper's. He lived in a great barn-like building in the centre of the town. His house was stored with boxes of all shapes and sizes. When he heard what Roger wanted he took him inside at once. Roger stared at the great boxes everywhere. He saw that some contained railway-lines, some bricks, some farms ready to be put together.

The store-keeper pulled out a box and pushed it to Roger. 'This will build a nice little house for one night,' he said. 'Don't lose any parts because I may want it back.'

Roger managed to carry the box on his back. It was very big and heavy. He balanced it on his car, and then found that he couldn't possibly get in himself.

'Tell me where to go and I'll push the car along,' he said to the doll. So she told him, and Roger guided the car from outside and at last came to a small field.

'This will do nicely,' said the doll. So Roger put the box down on the ground and opened it. It had inside a great many small wooden bricks with little pegs to hold them together. Roger had had a building-set like that before, so he soon set to work. It was fun building a toy house that was nearly as big as a real shed!

Before he had done very much the doll said she was hungry. She gave Roger some cardboard money, and he set off to the little shops. He bought some strange-looking cakes and pies, which really felt like painted wood, but which tasted most delicious when he and the doll tried them.

Then he went on with his building and before tea-time had finished the toy house. It was very good indeed, and the doll was delighted with it.

'Now you can go and ask at that big doll's house over there if they can spare us two beds, a table, and chairs for the night,' she said to Roger. 'You *will* stay with me till my leg is mended, won't you? Then you can take me back in your car tomorrow.'

Roger promised that he would. He hoped his mother wouldn't worry about him, but he didn't feel he could leave the doll with the broken leg. He went off to the big doll's house and found that the doll who lived there was a cousin of the broken-legged doll – so she was very pleased to lend the furniture they wanted. She sent two friends over with it, and soon the little house that Roger had built began to look very real and cosy.

The two of them had tea together. Then Roger went out to have a look round Toytown. This really was an adventure, and he wanted to see everything! The market was crowded with people and toys of all kinds. Clockwork mice ran busily about, and little tin men on bicycles rode up and down the streets, sometimes stopping and asking passers-by to wind them up again. Roger wound up a duck on wheels and a clockwork clown who went along head-over-heels all the time.

The animals in the market were all like toy farm animals, and they made as much noise as real ones. After he had looked at them all Roger made his way to the railway station. This was a most exciting place! Clockwork trains rushed in and out, and toy signals went up and down all by themselves. Toys got in and out of the carriages, gave up their tickets, and behaved just like people. Roger wished he could have a ride in one of the trains, but he didn't like to in case it took him too far away.

He went back at last to the little house he had built. The doll was in bed and asleep. Roger got into bed too, wondering if his mother was missing him, and very soon he was fast asleep. He didn't wake up until he heard the doll hopping about on one leg, getting breakfast.

'Hurry up!' she cried. 'I'm getting so excited to think I'll have my leg mended soon. Eat your breakfast and we'll go.'

Soon they were in the little car once more, and Roger drove to the hospital. He helped the doll inside, and the nurse, who was another doll, dressed in an apron and cap like a nurse, told him to wait. He sat down and watched the one-legged doll go hopping out of the room, carrying her broken leg carefully in her arms.

A great many toys came to be mended while he was there. A doctor stood at one end of the room and looked at all the patients one by one. There was a teddy bear whose boot-button eyes had come loose. They were soon sewn on tightly. There was a poor little duck that had lost its clockwork key. The doctor fitted it with another and it ran off happily. There was a red dog without a tail and a blue rabbit with only one ear. The doctor sewed a new tail and a new ear on, and off they went, as happy as could be. Roger thought he could watch all day.

And then a monkey came running in – and now Roger stared! For it was his own toy monkey from home. The long-tailed creature pointed to a hole in his back, from which the sawdust was beginning to come out. Roger went red. He remembered quite well that he had caught Monkey on a nail by accident and had torn it. He had meant to ask his mother to mend him and had forgotten.

The doctor sewed up the hole quickly. The monkey was very grateful. Roger screwed himself up in his corner, to hide. He didn't want the monkey to see him there. He might tell the doctor that there was the boy who had caught him on a nail! The monkey skipped gaily out without seeing him.

Then the doctor came over to Roger, with a big needle and cotton. 'What's the matter with *you*?' he asked, kindly. 'Where do you want to be mended? Shall I sew you up somewhere? Or have you lost your key?'

'No, I'm quite well, thank you,' said Roger, half-afraid the doctor might really sew him up somewhere. 'I'm just waiting for a friend of mine.'

At that moment in came the doll. She danced in on two legs, singing a little song of happiness.

'See!' she cried, dancing a tiptoe dance. 'My leg is mended, Roger! Isn't it lovely! Oh, I do hope Mary never drops me again. I might not find a kind little boy like you again, to take me to Toytown. Come along. We'll go home now!'

They climbed into the car again and off went Roger, hooting through the busy streets of Toytown. They soon left them behind and came to the wood where Roger had found the little doll.

'You can leave me here, Roger,' said the doll. 'I can find my way home easily now. Thank you so much for all your kindness. I hope I see you again one day.'

She threw her arms round his neck, gave him a good hug, then jumped out of the car and ran into the wood, waving her hand merrily. Roger drove on and at last came to the lane that led to his home. He drove up to the door and got out.

'Hello, Roger!' said his mother, coming to the door. 'You haven't been long! It's just about dinner-time.'

'Haven't been long!' said Roger in surprise. 'But, Mummy, I've been away a day and a night. I've been to Toytown.'

'You've been gone just an hour,' said his mother, kissing him. 'Go and wash your hands. You must have been dreaming!'

Well, wasn't that odd? Roger really couldn't understand it at all. *Had* he been dreaming? Or was time quite different in Toytown? He couldn't make up his mind what to think.

But one day he went to see his cousin Mary, who lived at a farm about two miles away – and there he saw the doll again! He was quite sure it was the same doll he had taken to Toytown, though now she was smaller.

'Mary, did your doll ever break her leg?' he asked his cousin. Mary nodded her head in surprise.

'Yes, I dropped her once,' she said. 'How did you know? But, Roger, it was so strange, her leg got mended all by itself somehow. One day it was broken – and the next it was all right again. I can't think how!'

'Well, *I* can tell you!' said Roger, proudly. And he told Mary all about his adventures in Toytown with the doll. She *was* surprised. She picked up the doll and looked at her.

And Roger saw the doll smile at him, though Mary didn't. So he *knows* his adventure really did happen, after all!

Poor Old Scarecrow!

There was once an old scarecrow who stood in the middle of a farmer's field. The farmer had made the scarecrow, and really, he looked very life-like. He had a turnip for a head, with eyes and mouth scooped out, and a piece of stick for a nose. He had an old bowler hat on his turnip head. Round his neck was a red scarf full of holes.

He wore a dirty old coat of the farmer's and a pair of trousers so ragged that, really, it was a marvel they hung together. But they did. He had two sticks for legs and two sticks for arms, and that was all there was of him.

He stood in the field on the sloping hillside, and looked in front of him all day long. The birds were not a bit afraid of him except when the wind blew his coat and scarf about. Then they thought he was alive and flew off, frightened.

'Silly creatures!' thought the scarecrow, scornfully. 'Frightened by a bit of flapping in the breeze. Oh, dear me, what a life this is! Nothing ever happens. All I see are the foolish birds and a lolloping rabbit or two. I want somone to talk to. There are many things I think about as I stand here all day long. Surely I am not too ugly for other creatures to speak to me. What about the pixies in the hedge? Why don't they pass the time of day with me sometimes? Are they too high and mighty?'

The pixies were not too high and mighty, nor were the goblins who lived in the caves along the hillside. But they were afraid to visit the scarecrow. You see, he really was so ugly, so dirty, so ragged! So they kept away from him, and even when he beckoned to them with his stick-like hand they pretended not to see him.

Now one night something very exciting happened to the scarecrow. It was like this. He stood out there in the middle of the field, yawning and bored. It was cold and he was lonely. Only a rabbit had come near him that day, and he really was longing to talk to someone.

So when he saw two strange figures walking over his field, he was very much excited.

'They are coming to visit me!' he thought. 'At

last I shall have someone to talk to! How marvellous!'

But when the two people came nearer in the pale moonlight the scarecrow saw that they were almost as ugly as he was! They were witches, long and lean, bony and bent.

'Let us talk here,' said one witch to the other. 'No one will hear us, in the middle of this lonely field. We will sit down beside the scarecrow and whisper our secret plans.'

'What a scarecrow it is, too!' said the second witch, scornfully, looking the poor scarecrow up and down. 'Turnip head and turnip brains! Silly, gaping thing!'

The scarecrow was so hurt and surprised at these unkind words that he couldn't think of anything at all to say. He just stood and gaped all the more, and he felt as if his scarf was choking him.

The witches took no more notice of him. They sat down on the cold earth and began to whisper.

Now the scarecrow's ears were not much to look at, but they were very sharp, so he could hear every word that was said. And very strange was the thing that the witches talked about on that moonlit night.

'The Princess comes this way tomorrow night,' whispered the first witch. 'She will only be attended by two fairies, and she will be in her rabbit-carriage.'

'Then we will lie in wait for her under the blackberry hedge over there,' whispered the other witch. 'We will take her prisoner and throw the fairies with her into the nearest holly bush.'

Both the witches laughed at this. The scarecrow was so amazed at what he heard that his hat fell off. Both the witches jumped up in alarm, and when they saw it was only the scarecrow's hat that had made them jump, they stared at the scarecrow angrily. The first witch picked up his hat and jammed it down so hard on his turnip head that it went over one of his eyes so that he could hardly see. But he didn't say a word. No, he knew better than that!

'No one knows of our plan,' said the first witch. 'Meet me here tomorrow night, friend, before the moon rises, and we will go to the hedge to lie in wait for the Princess.'

They went silently down the hill together, their pointed hats showing up in the moonlight, two strange and ugly figures. The scarecrow blinked his turnip eyes and thought hard about what he had heard.

He wondered who the Princess was who was coming that way the next night. So when he saw a small rabbit venturing into the field to eat a few shoots, he called to him in his funny woodeny voice:

'Rabbit! There is something important I must say to you. Come nearer.'

The rabbit looked at the scarecrow in alarm. He lolloped just a little nearer and cocked his long ears up at the scarecrow.

'Don't flap your coat at me,' he said, 'or I shall run away.'

'Don't be silly,' said the scarecrow impatiently. '*I* don't flap it. It's only the wind. Listen, rabbit. Who is the Princess who is coming this way tomorrow night?'

'It's the Princess Peronel of Pixieland,' said the rabbit in surprise. 'However did you hear that news, scarecrow? Why, we thought only the rabbits knew, because two bunnies that pull the carriage told us. Don't you tell anyone, now!'

'There's no need to,' said the scarecrow. 'Lots of people seem to know! There were two witches here just now, and they said that . . .'

But the rabbit didn't wait to hear any more. At the mention of the word 'witches' he was off like a shot! Witches! Tails and whiskers, to think that he was out on a night that witches chose! Ooh!

The scarecrow looked at the running rabbit angrily. *Now*, what was he to do? Just as he was telling the rabbit, so that he might be able to lollop off and warn the Princess, the silly little creature must needs run away as if a hundred dogs were after him!

'Hi!' called the scarecrow, in despair. 'Hi! Come back! I've got something very important to say.'

But the rabbit had disappeared into a hole and had warned all the other rabbits that witches were about. So not a single rabbit showed itself again that night, and the scarecrow shouted himself hoarse.

He began to get alarmed. Just suppose he couldn't get help in time? Just suppose the little Princess Peronel should really be taken prisoner by those two horrid witches! Just suppose – but the scarecrow really couldn't suppose any more.

When the sun rose, the birds came flying into the field. 'Perhaps if I call and beckon to them they will listen to what I have to say,' thought the scarecrow.

So he began to call to the birds in his hoarse,

woodeny voice, and he flapped his arm-sleeves about to beckon them and waggled his trouser legs.

But, dear me, the birds came no nearer – no, they were frightened, and flew away at once, screeching: 'The scarecrow is alive today! Beware! Don't go near him! He'll be walking down the field next!'

The scarecrow listened to their calls, and then a sudden thought came to him. He never *had* tried to walk, but just supposing he could? If he managed to walk down to the rabbit-holes he could give the warning easily then. He could shout it down the burrows.

Now, you know, scarecrows are so stiff that they cannot usually put one leg in front of another. But our scarecrow began to try. He had all the day in front of him, so he had plenty of time.

First he tried to pull a leg out of the ground. How he tried! How he tugged, how he pulled!

It was no good at all. He couldn't seem to move his leg at all. The farmer had driven the stick-legs firmly into the ground, and it was more than the poor scarecrow could do to move them. He was really in despair.

He stood gazing in front of him, feeling hot

and out of breath, when he saw a peculiar thing. Not far from him he saw a little mound of earth rising. Then another. Then another. Whatever could that be?

He soon knew. A little velvet mole came peeping out of the ground, but when he spied the scarecrow nearby he gave a squeal of fright and made as if he would dive back into the earth again.

'Mole, mole, don't go,' begged the scarecrow. 'I won't hurt you. I really won't. Listen, two witches are planning to take the Princess Peronel prisoner tonight. Will you go and warn the rabbits?'

'What is a witch?' asked the mole. 'And what is a Princess? Are they things to eat? I should like to hear of some nice new beetles to hunt for.'

'No, they're not things to eat,' said the scarecrow, in despair. 'Oh, you silly little mole, never mind what they are. Just go and give my message to the rabbits. It's important.'

'Nothing's important but food,' said the mole. 'I'm sorry, scarecrow, but I can't go out of my way to tell a silly message I don't understand. You'd better be careful, because I may have to tunnel right under you, and if I loosen the earth around your legs, you may tumble over. Ho ho!'

The scarecrow listened – and a bright idea flashed into his turnip head. Of course! That was just what he wanted! If only he could get his wooden legs loosened from the earth, he would be free to walk!

'Mole, tunnel right under me!' he begged. 'Do. Do!'

'You'll fall on your nose!' chuckled the velvet mole. 'You will! How I shall laugh!'

'Yes, you do it and laugh!' begged the scarecrow. 'It is sure to be funny. Go on, mole.'

So the mole dived back again into the earth and began to tunnel at top speed towards the scarecrow, throwing up mounds of earth as he went. Very soon the scarecrow felt the mole at work round his wooden legs and he knew that the earth was becoming very loose there.

The sun sank down. Darkness came over the field. The birds went to roost in the trees and in the ivy. Still the mole worked around the scarecrow's legs, trying to make him fall down on his nose. And at last down he went, flop! His hat rolled off and a large piece of earth went into his right eye.

But did the scarecrow mind? Not a bit! He

was as glad as could be.

'Ho ho ho!' laughed the mole, and went on his way to tell all his friends what a joke he had played on the scarecrow.

The scarecrow tried to pick himself up, but it was very difficult. He tried and he tried. The night grew darker and the scarecrow felt frightened. Suppose he couldn't get down to the rabbit-holes before the moon rose? It would be too late to warn everyone then, for the Princess would be taken prisoner before the moon came!

At last he managed to pick himself up! How strange he felt with his legs out of the ground! He picked up his hat and put it on.

And then he got a shock – for he saw creeping along by the hedge at the bottom of the field, the two witches! Yes, there was no mistaking their tall pointed hats.

'Too late, too late!' groaned the scarecrow in dismay. 'Oh, dear, oh, dear! The rabbit-carriage will be by at any minute now!'

He tried to stagger along down the field and, dear me, once he got going, he couldn't stop! The field was steep and the slope took his legs along very fast indeed.

Suddenly he heard a scream, and he knew what had happened. The rabbit-carriage had come along with the Princess and her attendants, and the two witches had stopped it. Down the field staggered the poor old scarecrow, and as he went, he yelled at the top of his voice:

'Beware, you bad witches! Here comes the great wizard Boolamoolahippitty-twink with his scratching nails, his pointed teeth, and his terrible spells! Oooooooooooh! Beware! I come, I come, the terrible wizard Boolamoolahippitty-twink!'

What made him call out all this he really didn't know, but he felt that he must try to frighten the two witches somehow.

And he certainly did!

When they heard this strange song coming out of the darkness, and saw, with their green witches' eyes, the queer, stumbling figure of the scarecrow, with his bowler hat on all crooked, and his scarf flying out behind him, they felt quite sure it *was* a wizard. They had never heard of the wizard called Boolamoolahippitty-twink, and no wonder, for there was no such person – but they quite thought it must be some fearfully powerful magician, and they were frightened almost out of their lives.

They screamed loudly, jumped on the two

broomsticks they had nearby, and sailed away into the sky at top speed. How glad the scarecrow was! He looked about for the Princess Peronel. There she was lying on the grass, looking as scared as could be.

'Princess,' said the scarecrow, in his hoarse, woodeny voice, 'Princess, I've come to . . .'

'Oooooh!' shrieked the poor Princess, in fright. 'Go away, you horrid wizard! I'd rather have the two witches than you! Go away!'

'But I'm not *really* a wizard,' said the scarecrow, humbly. 'I'm only a scarecrow, and I must beg your pardon, Princess, for daring to come near you, ugly old creature that I am. But you see, I *had* to rescue you from those horrid witches. I couldn't get anyone else to help.'

The Princess sat up and looked closely at the scarecrow. She saw his funny round turnip face, his stick of a nose, his wooden legs and arms, and his ragged old clothes – and she knew he wasn't a wizard, but only a poor old scarecrow. Very soon he had told her everything, and she listened in silence.

'You must forgive me for frightening you like this,' said the scarecrow. 'I know I am not fit to come near such a beautiful creature as yourself, Princess – but, you see, there was nothing else

I could do, was there?'

The Princess went up to the scarecrow. She put her warm little hand through his wooden arm and squeezed it hard.

'I think you're a darling!' she said. 'You are a dear, brave, clever old scarecrow, and I want you to come to Pixieland with me and be *my* scarecrow! I grow fine peas there all the year round and the birds do steal them so. But if you are there, the peas will be safe. Will you come?'

Would he come! The scarecrow couldn't believe his ears! He couldn't believe his eyes! To think that this should have happened to him, an ugly old scarecrow! Well, well, wonders never cease.

He found his voice at last.

'I'd love to come, Princess,' he said. 'But I can't. No, I can't, it's no use.'

'But why not?' asked the Princess in surprise.

'Because I'm too dirty,' said the scarecrow, mournfully. 'Much too dirty, and too ragged. I'd be ashamed to come to Pixieland like this.'

'Oh, is that all that is worrying you?' asked the Princess, with a laugh. 'How silly of you!'

She touched him lightly with her wand – and a strange thing happened. The scarecrow's bowler hat turned to gold. His scarf became red silk. His coat was made of thick brown satin with a thread of gold running through it, and his trousers turned to bright silver. My, he looked a real prince!

His turnip face was bright with joy as he saw all these wonderful things. The Princess touched him again.

'This is to make you able to walk and run like ordinary people,' she said. At once the scarecrow found himself able to walk to and fro without staggering and stumbling. He was full of delight.

'Oh, Princess!' he said, kneeling down before her, his wooden legs bending quite easily beneath him. 'You are too kind. Yes, I will come to be the scarecrow in your pea-patch. I shall be proud and honoured to scare away the birds for you. I shall walk all over your pea-patch and shout and wave my arms. Not a single pea of yours shall be eaten!'

'Well, that's settled, then,' said the Princess, pleased. 'Now, scarecrow, you shall come straight to Pixieland with me now. Look, there are my two fairy attendants with my rabbit-carriage. Go and bring them here, and you shall drive me home.'

Very proudly, full of joy, the scarecrow drove

the Princess and her two attendants home to the palace. Everyone thought that he must be at least a Prince, so magnificent did he look in his grand clothes. It was only when they saw his turnip head and wooden legs and arms that they saw he was really a scarecrow.

Now he lives in the garden of the Princess Peronel, King of the pea-patch. The birds are frightened of him and never eat a single pea, which pleases Peronel very much. You should see the scarecrow walking up and down, waving his arms and shouting at the birds! He is so proud and so happy – but he did deserve his good luck, didn't he?